AHDAF SOUEIF

I Think of You

Ahdaf Soueif was born in Cairo. She is the author of
the bestselling novel *The Map of Love*, which was short-
listed for the Booker Prize in 1999, as well as *Mezzaterra: Fragments from the Common Ground* and the novel
In the Eye of the Sun. She also has translated from the
Arabic the award-winning memoir *I Saw Ramallah* by
Mourid Barghouti. She lives with her family in London
and Cairo.

Also by AHDAF SOUEIF

Fiction
In the Eye of the Sun
The Map of Love

Nonfiction
Mezzaterra: Fragments from the Common Ground

Translations
I Saw Ramallah: A Memoir by Mourid Barghouti

I Think of You

I Think of You

STORIES

AHDAF SOUEIF

Anchor Books
A Division of Random House, Inc.
New York

FIRST ANCHOR BOOKS EDITION, MARCH 2007

The stories "Knowing," "1964," and "Returning" were originally
published in the book *Aisha* by Jonathan Cape, Ltd in 1983. The stories
"Mandy," "Satan," and "I Think of You" were originally published in
the book *Sandpiper* by Bloomsbury Publishing Plc in 1996. The story
"Chez Milou" was originally published by *SohoSquare* in 1988. The story
"Melody" was originally published by the *London Review of Books* in 1988.
The story "Sandpiper" was originally published by *Granta* in 1994.

Excerpt from "Sandpiper" from *The Complete Poems 1927–1979*
by Elizabeth Bishop. Copyright © 1979, 1983,
by Alice Helen Methfessel. Reprinted by permission
of Farrar, Straus and Giroux LLC.

"Have I the Right" words and music by Howard & Blaikley. Copyright
© 1964 by Ivy Music Limited. Used by permission of Music Sales
Corporation. All Rights Reserved.
International Copyright Secured.

The Cataloging-in-Publication Data is on file at the Library of Congress.

Anchor ISBN: 978-0-307-27721-3

Book design by Mia Risberg

www.anchorbooks.com

Printed in the United States of America
10 9 8 7 6 5 4 3 2 1

The world is a mist. And then the world is
minute and vast and clear. The tide
is higher or lower. He couldn't tell you which.
His beak is focused; he is preoccupied,

looking for something, something, something.
Poor bird, he is obsessed!
The millions of grains are black, white, tan and grey,
mixed with quartz grains, rose and amethyst.

—Elizabeth Bishop, "Sandpiper"

CONTENTS

Knowing

I remember a time of happy, dappled sunlight. French windows open onto a flowering garden. From the garden gate to the open windows runs a paved and sloping pathway, and at the top of the pathway stands a bright blue tricycle poised for the dizzying, exhilarating glide down the path. All you had to do was get it to the beginning of the incline and lift your feet off the ground and *whoo*—away you went. You had to pull up smartly or you ended up inside the living room.

The living room has huge, faded armchairs and colored rugs and lots and lots of books. The walls are covered with them. Some have pictures, some you are allowed to pick up and look at, some are not to be touched. All are to be treated with great respect and never torn or folded or scribbled in or put face downward or looked at while eating in case you drop food on them. In the middle of the books sit the grown-ups.

The grown-ups are wonderful. They drink tea and smoke and laugh and talk all the time. The women are beautiful with red lips and fingernails. The men are tall and handsome. They all do clever things. They write books and make music and paint pictures. Their pictures blaze on the walls of our apartment.

Looking back, I see a pool of sunlight, and in it, a child. She is dressed in a blue-and-white-spotted frock with a white lace bodice. She holds on to her mother's skirt. Seized by a sudden fit of shyness outside the door of the living room, she sucks slowly at her thumb. But then, coaxed and encouraged, she ventures in and is immediately picked up and cuddled and kissed to a chorus of "Darling." "I've got to paint her. I've simply got to paint her," cries Uncle Sameer, as he does every time and, reassured, she tosses her hair back and smiles up at him. Yes. The grown-ups are wonderful.

And clever. And wise. They can do anything, explain everything. The child is lying in her bed. Every time her mother puts out the light a horrible creature with long curving arms appears on the ceiling of her room and she screams. Her mother comes back in and switches on the light, but she can see nothing. After a bit she calls the father. He too can see nothing, but he lies down beside her. Her mother switches off the light and closes the door. He sees the creature on the ceiling. "It's the shadow of the chandelier, little goose." He comforts her and shows her how it moves when the chandelier moves and explains about light and shadow. She is safe.

Yes. The world is safe and pleasant and the worst grief I know is to be beaten at Snakes and Ladders by Uncle Murad. He moves my counter slowly down every curve of the final fatal snake and I watch, lips trembling, on the verge of tears, till my father intervenes and carries me off.

My father is a psychologist. He is very strong. He can crack nuts by pressing them in his hands. When we play in the garden he can run very fast. He runs very fast in circles. He runs so fast that I can't catch him. But after a bit he slows down and I am able to run up to his legs and hold him tight.

The garden is always sunny. I play with my blue tricycle or eat my meals sitting in a wide-eyed rocking duck. This is my home. I know the address by heart.

Near my home there is the club. My nanny, Dada Zeina, takes me there most afternoons. In summer I swim. At other times I play on the swings. Sometimes I have a magazine or a picture book. I sit on the grass beside Dada Zeina and look at the pictures. She chats to the other nannies, but I am absorbed in the pictures.

In an older part of town there is another house that I go to often. There too I know the address by heart. It is older than our house and the rooms are bigger and higher. In the center of a high-ceilinged room full of sunlight, a woman is kneeling on a red and blue prayer mat. Her hands are folded one over the other. Her eyes are closed. When they are open they are a deep green. Underneath her flowing white headdress, her hair is a long, soft light brown. Beside the prayer mat, the slippers she has taken off stand side by side. They are flat and made of crinkly pink leather with a tiny rosette on each toe. I sit close by on the floor solemnly watching the familiar ritual. This woman is my grandmother. My mother's mother. "Mama Hajja," I call her: Mama who has gone on the pilgrimage to Makkah. It is a title of respect. But it is also a truthful description. For Mama Hajja has been to Holy Makkah. Although she was delicate and her health was frail, she had gone. She had traveled alone, my grandfather (her husband) having had neither the time nor the inclination to accompany her and look after her. Her lips move as she nears the end of the Qur'ānic verses she is reciting and she slowly bends over to prostrate herself, her forehead touching the floor between two open palms. The broad, loved back is too great a temptation and I steal up from the floor and clamber onto it. Mama Hajja makes no sign that anything untoward has happened. When it is time, she slowly straightens up. I try to hang on but tumble off her back and onto the floor behind her. I wait. I know that soon it will be time for the second prostration. Sure enough, within a minute she bends over, forehead touching the floor, and in a flash I am again on her back. She recites "Praise be my Lord, most great" three times slowly, then slowly straightens, tumbling me once more off her back. I settle on the floor behind her. She recites the final Greeting to God and Muhammad, and his family and children and all the prophets that God had ever sent. She turns her head to salute the angels at her right and left shoulders and, almost in the same movement, reaches for her slipper. She stretches an arm behind her back and makes a grab for me, but I am small and quick and crouch just out of her reach, laughing. She turns and starts for me, in her hurry and irritation forgetting to stand up but coming after me on hands and knees, brandishing a pink slipper. I dart away, reeling with laughter and pointing my finger back at her, and suddenly she sits back on her heels on the sun-flooded polished wooden floor and starts to laugh too. I wait a few seconds to make sure it's safe, then rush back to fling myself into her open arms. "You little monkey. You would have made me break my prayers?" I snuggle contentedly against her breast in the sunlight, sucking my thumb. In my parents' house naughtiness is frowned upon. So is sucking your thumb. I name this other one the Spoiling House.

Now it is a sunny winter's day and I am playing in my grandfather's shop. It is a prospering furniture shop with his name, Morsi, emblazoned in gold Diwani script across the front. It stands on Morgan Street, the street forming the western border of the central marketplace in old Cairo. The market is a fascinating place with its high glass ceiling, its stacks of vegetables and pyramids of oranges, guavas, and Lebanese apples. It is slightly frightening too, with thousands of slaughtered chickens hanging open-beaked above the live ones who continue to scurry around, clucking mindlessly. The gutters between the stalls run with mud and blood, but people sit on little wooden stools drinking sweet tea and swishing the flies away with graceful horsehair flyswatters.

I am not allowed to go into the marketplace on my own, but I have the run of my grandfather's shop. The furniture on the ground floor is arranged for display. Gilt armchairs standing in a circle make a drawing room in the shop window and I sometimes sit here for hours gazing at the world outside: the meat vans unloading in front of the marketplace, the carts trundling in with fresh vegetables from the villages. I stare out at the shoppers as they stare in at the gilt drawing room.

Upstairs there is a loft used for storing furniture. You go up a set of creaky wooden stairs without banisters. It is dark. There is one feeble lamp, but its circle of light serves only to make the place more ghostly. There is a well in the middle of the floor, and from it you can look down into the shop. This loft is paradise. The furniture is all tumbled together, and in the gloom I create caves under huge desks and labyrinthine castles in piled-up sofas. The only thing I am forbidden to do is get inside the cupboards. Occasionally I slip into one and sit, knees to my chin, huddled in a corner, feeling both frightened and brave. But I never dare close the doors and engulf myself in total darkness.

Above this loft, arrived at by a different stairway, is the workshop: huge marble-floored rooms filled with the smell of varnish and the blare of the radio. A broad, sunny terrace overlooking the marketplace; stacks of wooden armchairs and desks waiting to be polished; and all my grandfather's workmen: carpenters, upholsterers, and varnishers, who carry me on their shoulders and buy me sweets and Sport Cola.

I have been playing in the loft when I hear them call my name.

"Aisha! It's lunchtime! Come down!"

I run down the stairs just as the boy from the neighboring restaurant comes into the shop carrying a large, round brass tray shining in the sunlight. On it is a sheep's head festooned with parsley and surrounded by little dishes containing the various salads and dips. In one corner of the tray there are five round loaves of bread. In another there are three bottles of cola. There is only one empty plate. The boy puts the tray down on a table between my grandfather and his friend Sheikh Zayed.

"Got everything you want, Am Morsi?"

My grandfather checks that the bread is hot and the drinks are cold and nods, waving his hand to dismiss the boy. He is a man of few words.

I sit on a swivel desk chair with two cushions under me and Sheikh Zayed tucks a napkin around my neck. They put the empty plate in front of me. "In the name of God, the compassionate and the merciful." The two men start breaking up the sheep's head with their fingers. They shred off some lean meat and put it on the plate in front of me. My grandfather hands me a fork. I want to eat like them with my fingers, but I know it's not allowed. *I* must eat with a fork. They eat in silence, occasionally putting a tidbit on my plate or in my mouth. And we drink our cola and dip our bread in the salads.

My grandfather is a big man with graying hair and sharp black eyes. He has large workman's hands and a gruff voice. Myth surrounds him: how his father died when he was six and his uncles usurped his land; how he trekked from his village in Upper Egypt to Cairo at the age of seven and found work in the central market; how he built up his business and became fabulously wealthy; how he rejected the trappings of wealth and rode in overcrowded buses where a thousand pounds at a stroke were picked from his pocket. He does not pray and is not known to be religious. Nobody ever calls him Hajj or Sheikh. They use 'Am for respect instead. They say he is a hard man, but I, his first grandchild, do not find him so. I know that if I choose the right moment and dance for him, singing,

> I come from Upper Egypt
> Like my father before me,
> And my granddad too,
> He comes from Upper Egypt

his face will break into a wide smile and he'll give me a brand-new pound note.

Now we finish eating and the boy comes to take the tray away. He brings with him two nargilas: one for my grandfather and one for Sheikh Zayed. I love watching the coals glow red and the water bubble as my grandfather pulls on the mouthpiece. I wait: I know that in time he will offer it to me. After a few puffs he does, and I pull and pull but I can't make the water bubble. He laughs and brings out his snuffbox. It is beautiful, engraved silver glinting in the sunlight. He takes a pinch and offers me the box. I am delighted. I know what he expects and I am happy to play the clown. I take a pinch of snuff and put it to my nostril. After a second I break into three exaggerated sneezes and my grandfather and Sheikh Zayed burst out laughing. I jump down from my chair and my grandfather catches me and wipes my face with his large white handkerchief with the blue border.

By Abdin Palace, there is another house that I remember. And another set of grandparents. I don't go there as often as I go to Grandfather Morsi's, but when I do go, it is to stay a few days. There are no uncles here, only two aunts, and it is much quieter and darker than in the other house. Here, I call my grandmother Neina and I would not dream of climbing onto her back while she prayed. However, sometimes at night she will take the net off her hair and it will fall down her back long and soft, black threaded with silver. Then she will let me kneel on the sofa behind her, and brush it carefully and gently.

Yes. To everything there is an order and a pattern. And the pattern and the order are good. Time, from one birthday to the next, runs gently by, overflowing with an abundance of pleasures. If there are fears or griefs, they are minor and I am always able to be comforted by the grown-ups.

It is my birthday, I am five years old. In the morning I go with my grandfather to Groppi's to order a three-tier chocolate cake with colored sugar rabbits and five blue candles. I also get a bar of Swiss chocolate. In the afternoon I go out on an errand with my aunt Soraya and spot a cart loaded with wooden bathroom clogs. I want a pair. "No," says my aunt. "Daddy won't like it."

"But I can keep them in the Spoiling House," I say, already practicing subterfuge. Eventually she gives in and buys me a pair. "I want to wear them now."

"You can't wear them in the street. They're only for the bathroom."

"I've seen people wear them in the street." I look around. A little beggar girl is coming toward us wearing a pair. "There!" I cry. "There! She's wearing clogs!"

"But she's a little beggar girl," protests my aunt. It is no use: I am sitting on the pavement, unbuckling my shoes. I clatter proudly back to my grandfather's in socks and clogs. When evening comes I am surrounded by uncles and aunts and presents. My grandmother has made me a pink tulle bridal dress with a long veil and train. I wear it happily. But I also keep on my clogs.

Then there are all the festivals. On the Prophet's birthday the streets are filled with bright stalls selling sweets. Sugar knights on horseback for boys, sugar dolls for girls. The doll stands, arms akimbo, in a flared dress and a high bonnet of colored and silver paper. She has painted black eyes and eyebrows and red cheeks and lips and stands in glory on the sideboard till the ants get her and she crumbles into decay beside her knight.

And Ramadan lasts a whole month. A month of winter evenings spent around the fire cracking nuts and roasting chestnuts. A month of exotic sweets and communal breakfasting at sunset. Of waking up at four in the morning (even though I do not fast) to join in the last meal before daybreak. Later to be tucked up again with a fresh hot-water bottle. A month of playing with a colored lantern with a real lit candle inside and singing special songs with my nanny and aunts.

And at the end of the month comes the small Eid. So the last few days are dedicated to cake-making. My grandmother and the women of the family sit around on the floor in a circle, chatting. Between their knees they hold the large copper urns and in them they knead the dough for the cakes. They roll the dough into little balls and stuff each one with some dates. Then they flatten them and lay them on huge black oven trays. Each cake has to have a pattern engraved on it with special pincers, and this is where I join in. I crawl around the trays making patterns with my silver pincers. On a few I am allowed to draw faces. When the cakes are all done, the servants balance the huge black trays on their heads and carry them to the public oven.

For the Eid you always wear new clothes. They are specially made and on the eve of the feast they are laid out ready to be worn in the morning. The big Eid lasts four days. Weeks before it, Grandfather buys a sheep and it is tethered to the iron railings on the balcony. Going to my grandfather's house becomes extra special: there is the sheep to ride and play with. But then, on the eve of the Eid, they tell me to say good-bye to the sheep. They tell me he is going back to his mother. He has enjoyed playing with me, but now it is time for him to go home. I go to sleep in a huge bed with springs and a feather quilt and when I wake up he has gone. I miss him. But I agree: a sheep should be with his mother. And I am consoled by the new clothes and by the fireworks they buy me. Catherine wheels make brilliant arcs of light, torpedoes go off with a deafening blast, Snaps catch fire in your hand when you scrape one against the wall (only the wall of the back staircase, nowhere else), and sparklers throw off a breathtaking profusion of stars and moons.

Another main event in life is the yearly migration to Alexandria. In July the whole family packs beachwear and bundles into cars and we set off on the long desert road to the Mediterranean. In Alexandria there is a two-story wooden house standing in an acre of sandy ground with palm trees. This is the "chalet." It is where I live during July and August. It is a short walk to the beach and we stroll it in our swimwear. On the beach they set up brilliant parasols and deck chairs and rugs. My aunts teach me to swim. My father and uncle throw me to each other in the water, occasionally dousing me in the surf. On the days when my grandfather comes up from Cairo he teaches me to play backgammon on an intricate inlaid board. He teaches me the classic maneuvers and the set moves. And he gives me silver money when I beat him.

To everything there is an order and a pattern.

Parental decree forbids servants and relatives to tell frightening stories or threaten abduction by the ghoul or the bogey or the man with the skinned leg. So I grow up in ignorance of the more menacing figures of folklore. I know Cinderella well, and am repeatedly ecstatic as the glass slipper is fitted to her dainty foot; I have unbounded confidence in Clever Hassan, who always comes out on top; and I know that the real story of Little Red Riding Hood ends with her and her grandmother emerging triumphantly from the wolf's belly. The wolf is so overcome by this miracle that he is transformed into a domestic pet and they all live together happily ever after.

Divine Order. Evil is a passing naughtiness; mighty forces work for the good and all stories end happily.

I endlessly make up tales surrounding the pictures in the books I cannot yet read. I pore over a bookful of Rodin sculptures and my parents are delighted with the sunny little fables I produce. My life is woven into my tales and my tales become part of my life: aunts and uncles are characters in a storybook and Hansel and Gretel join me under the desk in my grandfather's shop. I invent characters who become my friends and perform a play with them to an assembled family audience. "The child has such a lively imagination," they say, and surround me with admiration and love.

My parents' books become increasingly fascinating. I pick up even the ones with sparse illustrations and ask questions: "Who is this?"

"A man called Vathek."

"Where does he live?"

"He's not real. He was invented by a man called Beckford."

"Where does *he* live?"

"He lived in the last century, in England."

My father's books are still out of bounds.

Then there comes a break. My mother is absent and I live in the Spoiling House. After many weeks I go on a long journey across the sea alone with my father. We land in a cold dark wet windy place with a lot of people and a lot of trains. We sit in a café drinking hot milk. Then my mother's face emerges out of the rain. She is wearing a light green raincoat. She runs into my father's arms and I embrace her legs. She bends to pick me up and she is laughing and crying at the same time.

Now I remember a new home. It is much smaller than the ones we've left behind and not so pretty. But there is a fire in the living room wall. Everything here is much colder, much darker than I'm used to. There is no one; no one except my parents. And I don't see very much of them, for I am sent to school. My parents are pleased that I find my feet and learn the new language so easily. I miss my aunts and uncles and grandparents. But now I like my new friends. I like sitting on the floor on a huge sheet of paper and painting gray castles and soldiers in red and black uniforms. I like cuddling up to Miss Eve at storytime. I like taking a goldfish home for the holidays. I miss the sun. But I like the evenings when I sit at my mother's feet in front of the fire. She reads and writes and I look at pictures. There are no sugar dolls, no Ramadan lantern, no Eid, and no sheep. But instead there is Father Christmas and a stockingful of presents.

A new routine is introduced: I am initiated into a semi-grown-up role. Once a week my parents go out in the evening and I am left on my own. My mother gives me my bath and my dinner, then tucks me up in bed with a hot-water bottle. Both my mother and father kiss me good night. A small night-light is left burning. I don't mind at all. I tell myself stories till I fall asleep. In the morning the brownie will have visited me and left a chocolate or a packet of sweets under my pillow. He always comes when my parents go out in the evening. He never forgets. I try to wait up for him but I always fall asleep.

One night after I've fallen asleep I am suddenly wide awake. I sit up in bed and there, by the wall, I see him. He is a cross between a tiny man and a hamster. He is running quickly, upright on two legs, and he wears a little green suit and hat. He has a human face with a black mouse snout and pointed pixie ears. I know instantly that it's the brownie and I sit very still so as not to frighten him away. Then I wonder about his gift. I slip my hand under the pillow, but there's nothing there. I twist around to look and make sure. Still nothing. When I look up, he has gone. I know he will be back with my present, so I sit up to wait for him. The next thing I know it is morning and my mother is waking me up. There is a bag of licorice under the pillow. Over cornflakes I tell my parents that I've seen the brownie. At first they smile; then as I describe the scene in detail, they start to look anxious.

"You couldn't have, dear."

"But I did."

"You must have dreamt it."

"But I was *sitting up* in bed. I wasn't asleep."

"You couldn't *really* have seen the brownie."

"Why?"

"Because . . . well, because he can only come when you're asleep."

"But I *was* asleep. Then I woke up and he ran away."

They stop arguing with me but they still look uncomfortable and I cannot understand why.

An important event now takes place: I learn to read. One day, all of a sudden, the black marks around the pictures make sense and I am reading. Now every day on the way home from school, we stop at the public library and get me a book. Also, once a week I buy *Playhour* and *Robin*. I want to do nothing but read. I read and I read and I make up more stories. I go right through *Little Gray Rabbit* and *Noddy* and Hans Christian Andersen and my world is peopled with fascinating characters and bursting with adventure. Pinocchio and Squirrel go with me everywhere. I take to saving up my pocket money and buying comics. The brownie stops bringing me sweets and brings me books instead. Every book is a treasure trove and I play a part in every story.

One week I go to get my *Playhour* and am attracted by another comic. The cover shows a man in a black cloak and a beautiful blonde lady. The lady is tired, so he is carrying her and smiling. He has horrid teeth. Over the picture is written *Vampires.* I don't know what that means, but I already have a penchant for the romantic. I buy it. Something tells me my parents won't approve, so I smuggle it in and hide it among my toys till their next going-out night.

This time, not only don't I mind: I positively *want* them to go. When they do, I sit up in bed and read by the night-light: "The undead . . . those monstrous characters who feed upon the blood of the living . . . In Transylvania, Count Dracula's castle lay shrouded in blackest night." Here is new material indeed for my imagination. That night (after carefully rehiding the comic), I have a nightmare. An octopus is trying to catch me to drive a stake through my heart. I can see my mother, but she cannot see me or hear me scream. Luckily my parents have come home. They wake me up and comfort me and I tell them about the octopus but not about the stake. My father tells me that if I am afraid I'll dream of something, the thing to do is to remember it consciously before I go to sleep. Then I won't dream of it. For nights afterward I religiously intone "Octopuses and vampires, octopuses and vampires" before I go to sleep. It works. I don't dream of them. I also don't buy any more vampire comics.

My mother has a problem with me. I am finishing my books too quickly. We get home from school and long before bedtime I have finished the books from the library and am demanding more. In desperation she lets me browse among her books. I pick out a heavy red and gold volume of the *Arabian Nights*. "It's all right," she assures my father, "it's only the Lane edition." And I enter yet another new world. A world of Oriental souks and magic and djinnis. I am fascinated by the way djinnis can emerge from lamps, bottles, jars—in fact from anything. The world has undreamt-of possibilities. During the day I am at school and in the evening I am sunk completely into this firelit world of magic.

The week rolls around and it is going-out night again. I have my bath and my chicken soup and get into bed. My parents tuck me in and kiss me. I lie on my side in bed, gazing at the wall. The night-light is burning. Slowly, slowly, the wall begins to move. I stare at it. It splits down the middle and swings slowly and silently open. In front of my eyes appears a giant black djinni with a shaved head. All he wears is a Tarzan-like swimsuit in leopard-skin, and his bulging arms are folded across his bare chest. Behind him appears the vampire in the black cloak. He is grinning widely and his long teeth are dripping with blood. For long seconds I am mesmerized; then I unfreeze. In a flash I am out of bed and on the chest of drawers under the window.

My parents are still in the courtyard when they hear the sound of banging against glass. They turn and look up. A small figure in a white nightdress performs a demented dance behind the darkened windowpanes. Fists hitting at the glass, mouth wide open in a silent scream. They race back up the stairs, unlock the door, and rush in. I am still on the chest by the window as, hysterical, I explain what happened. They tell me it cannot be and try to laugh at me. But whatever they tell me is no use, for it *has* been and I have seen it. They are not able to explain it away.

My father sits in the living room and my mother comes and goes between us.

"I must go down now and you must go back to bed."

"No." I am hysterical and crying.

"Daddy says he'll be very cross with you."

"No."

"Daddy says there won't be any new toys or books till Christmas."

"I don't want any."

I know now my parents are neither omnipotent nor omniscient. They cannot stop the vampire from appearing, but at least they can be there when he arrives. I insist that they stay in and I win. I will not be left alone after this. And I am miserable.

1964

I stood in the snow, freezing and waiting for the bus. I was lonely. I had woken up at six as usual, washed and dressed in the cold dark while my young sister and brother slept on. I had poured myself some cornflakes, smothered them in sugar, and eaten them. Then I had let myself out of the back door and walked to the corner of Clapham High Street to wait for the No. 37.

The snow was deep around my ankle-high fur-lined black suede boots inherited from my mother. Or rather, I suppose now, donated by my mother while she wore ordinary shoes in the snow. Fourteen, with thick black hair that unfailingly delighted old English ladies on buses ("What lovely curly hair. Is it natural?") and which I hated. It was the weather; hours of brushing and wrapping and pinning could do nothing against five minutes of English damp.

I loved Maggie Tulliver, Anna Karenina, Emma Bovary, and understood them as I understood none of the people around me. In my own mind I was a heroine and in the middle of the night would act out scenes of high drama to the concern of my younger sister, who had, however, learned to play Charmian admirably for an eight-year-old.

We had come to England by boat. My father had come first. My mother had had trouble getting her exit visa. It was the New Socialist era in Egypt and there had been a clampdown on foreign travel. Strings were pulled, but a benign bureaucracy moves slowly and it was two months before we were allowed to board the *Stratheden* and make for England.

We got on at Port Said. The *Stratheden* had come through the Suez Canal from Bombay and before that from Sydney. It was full of disappointed returning would-be Australian settlers and hopeful Indian would-be immigrants, and beneath my mother's surface friendliness there was a palpable air of superiority. *We* were Egyptian academics come to England on a sabbatical to do *post*doctoral research. I wasn't postdoctoral, but it still wasn't quite the thing to play with the Indian teenagers, particularly as among them there was a tall, thin seventeen-year-old with a beaked nose called Christopher who kept asking me to meet him on deck after dark. In a spirit of adventure I gave him my London address.

I was summoned into my parents' room, where the letter lay on the desk. It was addressed to me and had been opened. It never occurred to me to question that. It said that it had been respectfully fun knowing me and could he meet me again? It had a passport-size photograph of him in it. My parents were grave. They were disapproving. They were saddened. How had he got my address? I hung my head. Why was it wrong to give him my address? Why shouldn't I know him? How had he got my address? I scuffed my shoes and said I didn't know. My lie hung in the air. Why had he sent me a photograph? I really didn't know the answer to that one and said so. They believed me. "You know you're not to be in touch with him?" "Yes." There were no rows, just silent, sad disapproval. You've let us down. I never answered his letter and he never wrote again—or if he did I never knew of it.

I was not troubled by the loss of Christopher, just by the loss of a potential adventure. Anything that happened to me represented a "potential adventure." Every visit to the launderette was brimful with the possibility of someone "interesting" noticing me. When I slipped and sprained an ankle, the projected visits to the physiotherapist seemed an avenue into adventure. But the old man massaging my foot and leering toothlessly up at me ("What a pity you don't slip more often") was more an ogre than a prince, and after one visit my ankle was left to heal on its own.

The likelihood of my actually arriving at an adventure was lessened by the eight-thirty P.M. curfew imposed by my parents ("Even in England it's not nice to be out later than that, dear").

But no path to rebellion was open to me, so I waited for something to happen obligingly within the set boundaries.

Days of calm Clapham harmony passed and I was fretting—"moping," my mother would say. Nothing ever happened. Life was passing me by. Then one day, when I returned from the launderette, my mother said that some young people, the vicar's children from down the road, had come by and asked if I would like to go out with them that evening. She had said yes for me. I was thrilled.

They came to collect me. Two tall and angular girls with vanishing eyebrows and hair pulled back into ponytails and a boy with extremely short hair and glasses and a brown-checked suit. My knowing heart made a little motion toward sinking, but I was resolute. I was going out with three young people of my own age. I did not know where we were going, but the possibilities were infinite. We might go down to the café at the end of the road and play the jukebox; I had looked through the window and seen it gleaming. We might go to a movie ("It's called a film, dear"). We might go to a youth club; I had heard of those and imagined them to be like the Gezira Club at home, only much more exciting and liberated. Instead, we went to church.

It was not even an old and picturesque church. It was modern and bare and the benches were miles away from the pulpit and my new friends' father preached for a long, long time. I told myself it was nice that they thought nothing of taking me, a Muslim, to their church. It was proof that I belonged—a little; that I wasn't as different as I feared I was. We all prayed.

———

I knew about prayers from books I had read and made the appropriate movements, and when we bent our heads and closed our eyes, communing silently with God, I prayed for something to happen to relieve the awful tedium of life. I knew it was slightly incongruous to ask for excitement in church, but I was desperate.

"Friends," the vicar said, "in our city today we find increasing numbers of people who come to us from far places: from alien races, alien beliefs. There are some of those among us tonight. Should any person in this congregation wish to join with us in the love of Jesus Christ, let them raise their hands now while the eyes of everyone are closed in prayer and I will seek them out later and guide them into the love of Our Lord. Raise your hand now." I kept my eyes closed tight and my fists clenched by my sides. I could not swallow. There was no doubt in my mind that he meant me.

Afterward we all had tea in a hall somewhere in the building. Everybody was large and pale with straight light brown hair and tweeds. I felt excessively small and dark and was agonizingly conscious of my alien appearance, and particularly my alien hair, as I waited to be sought out and guided into the love of Jesus Christ. Mercifully, it did not happen. Even so, I had been—however unknowingly—betrayed, and I knew I would never go out with the vicar's children again.

On the way home I kept my eyes open for the teddy boys and the rockers preening on the street corners. My heart yearned after them, with their motorcycles and their loud and gaily colored girlfriends. They were all that I was missing, and

every time I walked past one, my heart would thud in antici-
pation of his speaking to me. It was hopeless, I knew. My parents would never allow me to make friends with them. And
when a crowd of them whistled at me one day, I knew it was
even more hopeless than that. For they were hostile. And I
realized that with my prim manner and prissy voice they
wouldn't want me for a friend anyway. I was a misfit: I had the
manners of a fledgling westernized bourgeois intellectual and
the soul (though no one suspected it yet but me) of a rocker.

After I had refused a few times to go out with the church
children ("But you're always moping around complaining
you don't know anybody"), temporary rescue came from
some friends of my parents. We went to visit them and it
turned out that they had a son three years my senior. They
suggested (I was sure to his annoyance) that he take me to the
theater. My parents had no choice but to give their consent
there and then, and arrangements were made for later in the
week. Oddly, though, I still had to get formal permission to
be out late. Permission to go to the theater apparently did not
automatically include that. After all, one could always get up
in the middle of the first act and be home by eight-thirty.
However, permission was granted, but at ten-thirty on the
dot I had to be home. I bathed myself like a concubine and
went out dressed to kill in white gloves and a tartan kilt.
There were lots of awkward silences. *Hobson's Choice* ended at
ten. David suggested we have something to eat but I had to
get from Waterloo to Clapham in half an hour, so food was
out. There followed a rush to get home, and though he kissed

me good night in our front garden he never asked me out again. But I had had an adventure: my first-ever kiss. I had felt nothing at all, but I became more and more a heroine and borrowed from the library Mills & Boon romances that I read by flashlight under the covers in the dead of night.

By now my parents had decided that the best thing to do with me was send me to school. I was meant to be studying at home for my Egyptian preparatory certificate at the end of the year, but at school I would use all my time constructively. I would also meet people my own age and make friends. I looked forward to it. I had always been happy at my school in Cairo and had no misgivings about this one. Besides, schools in books like *The Girls' Annual* all seemed jolly good fun. Because of their liberal, enlightened ideology and that of their friends and advisers, my parents decided to put me in a comprehensive—in Putney.

So here I was. It was early '64. The Beatles yelled "I wanna hold your hand" and shook their long shiny black hair and their hips; the mods and rockers zoomed through the streets in their fancy gear; and I stood in the snow at the No. 37 bus stop, on the outside looking in.

My first contact with school was with the dark cloakroom lined with rained-on navy blue coats, berets, and boots.

My second was with the long, windy corridor you had to walk through without your coat to get to the main body of the school.

My third was with thousands of uniformed girls in a huge hall singing about fishermen.

No one had warned me it was a girls' school. I had always been in a mixed school at home and found boys easier to get along with than girls. Suddenly school didn't seem like such a good idea; a vast, cold place with thousands of large girls in navy blue skirts.

"You can be excused from assembly on grounds of being Mohammedan," whispered the teacher who had brought me there. No fear. I wanted nothing more than to merge, to blend in silently and belong to the crowd and I wasn't about to declare myself a Mohammedan or even a Muslim and sit in the hallway looking bored and out of it with the Pakistani girls wearing their white trousers underneath their skirts. "It's all right," I said. "I don't mind."

My attempts at fading into the masses were unsuccessful. During the first break I was taken to Susan, the third-form leader.

"Where you from?" She was slight and pale with freckles and red hair.

"From Egypt."

"That's where they have those pharaohs and crocodiles and things," she explained to the others. "D'you go to school on a camel?" This was accompanied by a snicker, but I answered seriously.

"No."

"How d'you go to school, then?"

"Actually, my school is very near where I live. So I simply walk." As I said this I was conscious of ambiguity (I even knew the word for it): I had not made it clear that even if

school were far away I still wouldn't go on a camel. I started
again: "Actually, we only see camels—"

"D'you live in a tent?"

"No, we live in a Belgian apartment block."

"A what?"

"An apartment block owned by a Belgian corporation."

"Why d'you talk like that?"

"Like what?"

"Like a teacher, you know."

I did know. I knew they were speaking Cockney and I was
speaking proper English. But surely I was the one who was
right. My instincts, however, warned me not to tell them that.

"How many wives does your father have?"

I bridled. "One."

"Oh, he don't have ten, then? What does he do anyway?"

"Both my parents teach in the university." A mistake this,
one I would live to regret; I was affiliated with the enemy
profession.

"Oh, teachers, are they?"

"In the *university*," I supplied.

"Sarah's dad's an engineer. He makes a hundred pounds a
week. How much does yours make?"

Sarah's dad was obviously the financial top dog in the third
form. But what was I supposed to say? Nothing, actually, he
lives on a grant? But don't you see, we're intellectuals, we're
classless? You can't ask me such a vulgar question?

"I don't know."

"Well, d'you have bags of money?"

I heard my mother's voice. "We spend our money on travel, books, records, on *culture* . . ."

This was met with silence. Then: "D'you have a boyfriend?"

Again I heard my mother's voice: "I know boys who are friends."

"D'you have a special boyfriend?"

I thought quickly. David hardly qualified as my boyfriend. But for status, I lied. "Yes."

"D'you kiss him?"

"Do I what?" I stalled. I didn't really want to share that. And something told me it would unleash other questions I wouldn't be able to answer.

"D'you kiss him?"

"No."

"D'you sit on his knee?"

"No."

"Well, how far have you got, then?"

"We went to the theater," I said. They lost interest at that point. Just moved on and never paid me much attention again. There was a girl there with blue eyes and straight black hair and her second name was Shakespear. I could have made friends with her, I thought. But she was Susan's best friend and I would not compete.

School was a disaster. The white girls lived in a world of glamour and boyfriends to which I had no passport. The black girls lived in a ghetto world of whispers and regarded me with suspicious dislike. I was too middle of the road for them. There was one girl of Greek parentage, Andrea. She came home with me one day. She came into our kitchen as my mother was preparing dinner. "Cor blimey!" she cried. "Olives. Can I have one?" Smiling kindly, my mother pressed her to take several. But to me she seemed unmitigatedly gross, and although I was polite to her, I could not make myself be her friend.

Academically, it wasn't much better. I only scraped through most subjects and was terrible at math. I couldn't understand why at the time because I was doing fine with the math I was studying at home on my own. Looking back, I realize it was because I didn't know the terminology in English. The teacher was a harassed, birdlike man in white shirtsleeves, with huge eyes swimming behind his rimless spectacles, and he looked so helpless that it never occurred to me to ask him for help.

As for brilliance, I could not have chosen an unluckier subject to excel in: English. The class would have forgiven me outstanding performance in science or sports, but English? And Mrs. Braithwaite, with her gray bun, her glasses over sharp blue eyes, her tweed suit hanging lower at the front than it did at the back, booming out, "The Egyptian gets it every time. It takes someone from Africa, a foreigner, to teach you about your native language. You should be ashamed." At first I was proud and thought how dumb they were not to know that birds of a feather "flocked together," that worms "turned," and that Shylock wanted his "pound of flesh." But as the hostility grew I realized I had made another mistake. I tried to fade into silence, but it was no use. Those sharp blue eyes would seek me out and she would call me by name, and I was not humble enough to give a wrong answer or say I didn't know.

Meanwhile, at break, I wandered around the cold playground, yearning for my sunny school in Cairo, and soon I learned to smuggle myself into first lunch, where I would quickly bolt down shepherd's pie and prunes and custard, then slink off to the library. There, hidden in a corner, holding on to a hot radiator uninterrupted by cold blasts of air or reality, I communed with Catherine Earnshaw or pursued prophetic visions of myself emerging, age thirty, a seductress complete with slinky black dress and long cigarette holder, a score of tall, square-jawed men at my feet.

At sports time, however, I was not so lucky. I clambered nimbly enough up and down ladders in the gym but we often had to go out onto the playing fields for games of hockey. Why hockey? I asked. Why not tennis or handball? No. Hockey was the school game and that was what we played. The weather was cold and gray and damp. The cold made my bones chatter, the gray depressed me, and the damp made my hair curl. The hockey sticks terrorized me. I had visions of them striking my ankles, my legs, bare and goosefleshed in my gym slip. I lurked on the sidelines, shivering and protecting my legs with my hockey stick. There was no escape. And it was too cold to dream.

My parents were satisfied. I could not admit failure or disappoint them by telling them I was miserable at school, so I dwelled on the treasures in the library and my achievements in the English lessons with a smattering of information on films we watched in history and geography. The rest, when questioned, came under the broad heading "Okay."

As a mark of approval, I was given a tiny Phonotrix tape recorder with which I taped songs from *Top of the Pops* and *Juke Box Jury.* I taped them through the microphone and the sound I got was terrible, but I could hear through the distortion and I played "Can't Buy Me Love" and "As Tears Go By" incessantly.

Music was magic to me, and every day as I walked home from the bus stop I would peer through the net curtains at the jukebox gleaming against the wall in the corner café. It was a dark, different world in there; there were square tables with plastic covers checkered in green and white. On each table were plastic pots of salt, pepper, mustard, and tomato ketchup. At the tables sat silent old men in cloth caps and jackets and shirts with no ties. One day I pushed open the door. There was a single chime and I walked in.

My heart was pounding and I couldn't see very clearly at first. The counter at the far end floated in a haze. I walked up. A large man in a striped apron stood behind it. I put a shilling on the counter and asked for a cup of tea. He pushed sixpence and a cup of tea back at me. I carried them over to a table in the corner and sat down. When I had got my breath back I stood up again and walked over to the jukebox and studied the titles. Here I was on familiar ground. I put in my other shilling and selected three records. I didn't drink my tea. It was strong and white and not like the tea I was used to at home. But I was happy. When the songs were over I walked out and went home. I never told anyone about my adventure. But every three days, when I had saved one and six from my pocket money, I stopped on the way home at the corner café, bought tea I never drank, and played the jukebox. The Beatles, the Stones, the Animals, Peter and Gordon, Cilla Black, the Swinging Blue Jeans, the Dave Clark Five. I played them all. And for the duration of three songs I was happy and brilliantly alive.

My secret bursts of life at the corner café sustained me, but at school things got steadily worse. The atmosphere in English was becoming intolerable and I could hardly believe my own stupidity at math and science. My hiding place in the library was discovered and I was often yanked out and deposited in the middle of the playground. My legs got knocked with the hockey sticks. The white girls lived their lives and the colored girls lived theirs and I hovered on the outskirts of both. Then one day the St. Valentine Dance was announced.

I was terror-struck and elated. All these girls would turn up in their designer clothes with their sophisticated boyfriends. They would glide with ease onto the dance floor and do the Shake. Would I be a wallflower? Unwanted? Again the odd one out? I never dreamed of not going. The world of glamour, passion, excitement, and adventure was going to be revealed for an evening. It was going to come within my reach and I would certainly be there to grasp it.

I got permission to go to the dance, and very special permission to stay out until eleven o'clock. I asked David, the only boy I knew in London, to come with me. My mother bought me my first pair of high-heeled shoes: *le talon bébé,* the style was called, and the heels were just one and a half inches high.

February 14th finally arrived. My hair was shining, my turquoise silk dress with the high Chinese collar was enchanting, and I had nylon stockings and high-heeled shoes. David came to fetch me in a dark suit and had a Pepsi with my mother before we left. He had borrowed his father's car, so we drove to Putney in style. I played it cool, as though, for me, every night was St. Valentine's night, but in my head was a starry, starry sky.

We got to school and made our way to the assembly hall. School was transformed. It was no longer dull and cold and hostile. It was vibrant, throbbing, every door, every corridor leading to the magical place where the dance was to be held.

It was eight o'clock as we walked into the hall. The lights had been dimmed and the loudspeaker was beating out "Come right back, I just can't bear it, I got some love and I long to share it," and nobody was on the dance floor. All the girls were there. They were in party clothes and stood grouped together at one end of the hall. At the other end, huddled in tight, nonchalant groups in dark suits, were the boys from Wandsworth Comprehensive, our sister school.

The situation slowly sank in. None of the girls had brought a boy with her. After all the brave talk about kissing and sitting on knees, no one had actually brought a boy with her. They were all standing there, tapping their feet and hoping that the boys from Wandsworth would ask them to dance.

And the boys were nervous, pretending they didn't know what they were there for and chatting to their mates.

We joined some girls from my class for a while, but conversation was awkward and we ended up standing alone by the wall. I tried to enjoy the music, but it felt dead and flat. David asked me to dance, but I knew he was being dutiful, and besides I was too shy to be alone with him on the floor.

Time passed as I hung on, waiting for something to happen while the evening slowly crumbled away and the stars went out one by one. I knew now there was no hidden world, no secret society from which I was barred. There was just—nothing.

A week later I stood as usual at the bus stop in the cold morning. I waited a few moments for the No. 37 then turned back and walked home. When my mother woke up she found me sitting in my school clothes in the kitchen with a fresh bowl of sugared cornflakes in front of me.

"Aisha! What's the matter? Are you ill?" she asked.

"No," I said.

"Well, what's the matter? Why aren't you at school?"

"I'm not going to school anymore."

"What?"

"I'm not going to school anymore."

"Have you gone crazy? What's the matter with you?"

"I'm studying for my Egyptian prep, aren't I? I'll concentrate on that."

"But why won't you go to school?"

"I don't want to."

"But why?"

"It's just not worth it."

"But you liked it so much—"

"I hated it."

"What on earth will your father say?"

". . ."

"He'll be very angry."

"I'm not going to school anymore."

She told my father. She carried back protests, even threats: "Daddy is terribly displeased with you," then, "Daddy won't speak to you for weeks." Withdraw all your love, I thought. I won't go back. They went against their principles: "You won't get any more pocket money." It was still no good.

Every morning my parents went to the university and my sister and brother to school. I would draw up my father's large armchair in front of the television, carry up some toast and butter, and watch the races. Or I would switch on my Phonotrix and dream. Or read. The whole house was my territory from nine in the morning to five in the afternoon and I lived my private life and was impervious to the cold, disapproving atmosphere that pervaded the evenings. After a couple of weeks they gave up.

One day I discovered a secret cache of books hidden in my parents' bedroom. *Fanny Hill, The Perfumed Garden* of Sheikh Nefzawi, and the *Kama Sutra*. My rebellion had paid off in grand style. I spent my fifteenth year in a lotus dream, sunk in an armchair, throbbing to the beat of the Stones, reading erotica.

And I passed my exams.

Returning

The little red car came speeding along the road and turned abruptly to park under a tree in front of a three-story house. Nobody got out. The engine did not die. Then the car moved again; it backed out of the parking place, made a sharp U-turn, and headed back the way it had come.

"I need those books," Aisha told herself. "I'm teaching a course and I need those books." She drove to the main street, then took a right turn. She drove straight on until she came to the roundabout. She circled the roundabout and came to a vast square. She knew she had come the right way, but she did not recognize this square. She remembered a green garden with spreading trees and flower-beds and paths of red sand. She saw

---

instead a construction site. In the foreground was a large, squat yellow mosque. On it was a placard, and on that in big green letters were written the words THE MOSQUE OF ISMAIL. She wondered who Ismail was and what degree of importance or wealth had got for him the planning permission to set up his mosque right here, in the middle of an area obviously designed as a recreation ground for the houses around it.

The red car went slowly up the east side of the square. Behind the mosque another building was coming up. The floors that had been completed were already graying as the rest were piled on top of them. A placard proclaimed the project: THE FIRST ISLAMIC INSTITUTE IN THE GOVERNORATE OF GIZA.

Between them, the Mosque of Ismail and the Islamic Institute took up five-sixths of the garden. Aisha looked at the strip that was left. The few trees were dusty and the grass was sparse and yellow. The whole place was strewn with bricks, cement, steel rods of varying lengths, and mounds of sand. There was no one about. It felt more like a demolition than a construction site. She wondered about the frogs they used to hear at night. And the crickets. Where had they gone? Had they all moved into the sixth of semi-garden that was left? And what did they do about territorial rights? How could they coexist in such a drastically reduced space? But then, maybe they didn't. Maybe the strong had overcome the weak and a race of superfrogs was now living in the remains of the garden. The builders of the Mosque of Ismail and the First Islamic Institute in the Governorate of Giza were helping evolution along.

The road was bumpy and dotted with potholes. Some of the potholes were full of stagnant water. Aisha looked around her. She remembered a bright winter day, a motor scooter wobbling under her as she tried to ride it down a smooth road. Finally it had collapsed on its side and she had fallen, one leg caught under the little Vespa. Everyone had run to her, but she had picked herself up and tried again. She looked around. You'd be mad to try to learn to ride a motor scooter down this road now.

She arrived at the top of the square. Six years ago their house had been the only one along the north side. Pretty, in five stories of reddish brown and beige, it had looked over the garden. Now it was flanked by tall apartment blocks and so stood diminished, looking bleakly out over the dusty road and the Pepsi-Cola kiosk that had sprung up on the pavement in front of it.

Aisha looked around for a place to park. There were no trees to cast any shade and one side of the road was much like the other. She pulled the car over to what used to be the curb and stepped out into a sand heap. She shook the sand from her shoes. The curious heads hanging out of windows were still there, but now a number of them were covered in the white Islamic headdress that was spreading so rapidly. Did they belong to the same people as six years ago? Or different? Younger sisters, perhaps, daughters? Out of the corner of her eye she could not tell. Ignoring them, as she had always done, she walked purposefully in.

The tall glass doors were still there. Miraculously they had not yet been broken. The marble-floored lobby was clean, but there were no plants in the pots and there were cigarette ends on the dry, cracked earth. A strange man in a striped galabiya was sweeping the marble floor. She wished him good day. He answered sullenly, leaning on his broom, waiting for her to pass.

"Are you the doorman here now?" she asked.

"God willing," he replied briefly.

"Where are Abdu and Amna?" she persevered.

"Abdu? They took him into the army long ago. And Amna has gone to live with her folk in the village."

"Oh."

She started climbing the stairs. She wanted to ask more. Had Abdu and Amna finally had their much-desired baby? Or were they still barren? What had Abdu done about learning to read? They had been incorporated into her dream of coming home, these two. She had even gone down to Mothercare and looked for Babygros for Amna's longed-for child.

Repeatedly she had imagined in detail the scene of her homecoming. It would be the beginning of the academic year, a warm October day. She would drive up to this door with Saif. Abdu would jump up and come running out, wearing his broad grin and his white peasant's underwear, his eyes and teeth shining in his dark face, crying, "Praise God for your safe return, Sitt Aisha!" He would grab her hand and try to kiss it while she protested and insisted on shaking his hand. "How are you, Abdu? How are you doing? And how is Amna?" And hearing the noise, Amna would look out from the room below the stairs and, seeing her, come out tying her colored kerchief around her hair, her slow, shy smile spreading over her pretty face. And she too would praise God for her safe return and ask, "Have you come to stay with us for good now?" And when Aisha answered yes, Amna would say, "You fill the house with light." They would carry her cases upstairs. They would all have to make two journeys because there would be a lot of luggage after such a long stay abroad. Later, she would unpack and come down to give Abdu and Amna their presents: for Amna a dress length of brightly patterned synthetic material with the trimmings and buttons to match, and for Abdu a watch. And if there should be a child . . .

She had arrived at her floor. The passage was dark. The old worn-out key was ready in her hand, but she could not see the keyhole. She reached out blindly and the key immediately fitted into the lock. Is it coincidence? she wondered. Did I just happen to find the lock? Or does my hand remember? She turned the key. It was a little stiff but the door opened. She felt a surge of irritation. Typical. Going away for two weeks and not bothering to double-lock the door. Then she remembered. It's nothing to do with me.

She pushed the door open and a forgotten but familiar smell met her. She stood still. It couldn't be. She had always thought it was the smell of fresh paint and that as the flat grew older it would vanish. For the year that they had lived in the flat it had constantly been there and she had thought, With time it will go. Time had come and time had gone and the smell was still there. Maybe he'd had the flat repainted? Her hand, moving along the wall, found the light switch. No, it had not been repainted. The walls were the same: olive green on one side, beige on the other. It must be a ghost smell, she thought. Like a ghost limb. When they cut off your legs you go on feeling the cramps in your toes. Only now they are incurable. I'm smelling fresh paint because I'm used to smelling it. It's not *really* here, but I'm smelling it.

Her eyes traveled along the entrance hall and fell on the white marble basin in the middle of the green living room wall. A sheet of cardboard had been laid across it and balanced on it were some telephone directories. What plans they had had for it. It was to be a small fountain, the wall behind it to be inlaid with antique ceramic tiles and its pedestal surrounded by plants in large brass urns. They had had to wait—a question of money. But the basin had been there. It was the very first thing they had bought for the house. Wandering down the old bazaar one day, they had found it thrown carelessly into the dusty corner of a junk shop. The owner had wanted ten pounds, but they had got it for eight. All three pieces: the basin, the back panel, and its pedestal. They had carried the heavy marble carefully to the car and later she had made inquiries about getting it scoured and polished. Someone recommended a shop in Taht el-Rab' and she had gone with her mother-in-law. When they got there it turned out that the man specialized in cleaning tombstones. Saif's mother had been shocked and urged her not to leave the basin with him. But she had laughed. No omen could dim her happiness, no headstone mar their future, and she had left the marble basin to be cleaned among the winged angels and the inscribed plaques. Later it had been fixed—with its beautiful shell-like back panel—into the green wall. And sometimes she had filled it with water and put in it a small machine that made a miniature fountain. It had always delighted their friends, and she had sat on the black rocking chair and watched it for hours.

She craned her neck. The rocking chair was there. In exactly the same position she had left it six years ago: angled by the French windows under the smaller bookshelves. A present from her white-haired professor of poetry, it had arrived three days after the wedding with a huge bouquet and had immediately become her favorite seat.

She stepped inside the flat and closed the door quietly behind her. It needed oiling. The handle was hard to turn. She faced the darkened flat and felt it tilt. She headed quickly left down the long corridor to the bathroom. She did not switch on the light but crouched in front of the toilet, retching. She wondered whether the cistern worked. It did. That had always been a good thing about the flat: they'd never had trouble with the plumbing.

Washing out her mouth she glanced up and saw her reflection dimly in the large mirror hanging beside her. She looked. It had been part of a Victorian hall stand which she had found in a junk shop and he had declared hideous. So they had compromised: the top and bottom of the stand had been cut away and disposed of, and the mirror with the intricately carved frame now hung suspended on the wall. She switched on the light, then went back to the mirror. The reflection staring back at her was not the one she was used to seeing there. The changes moved into focus. A slimmer face framed by shorter, more curly, though still black hair. A string of now-taken-for-granted pearls shone around her neck. She fingered the pearls. She remembered a hotel bedroom in Paris and the wonder and delight when the pearls were thrown into her lap as she sat up in bed. He had created Paris for her. As he had created Rome. Then he had stopped. Brussels, Vienna, Athens. They were all untouched by his magic. Why? They had still been together. She shook her head. Her expression too was different. The open, expectant look was gone. Instead there was—what? Repose? Something that people took for serenity. But she knew. She knew it was frail as an eggshell. She shook her head again and looked around. The shower curtains and matching bits and pieces had been bought in Beirut. Such a tight budget. And onion soup: her first taste of *soupe à l'oignon gratinée* eaten with melba toast in the Hotel Martinez at one o'clock in the morning as they'd planned their shopping list for the next day. She had loved it. The thin strands of the *gratinée* stretching as she pulled the spoon away from the dish, the melba toast crisply cutting through them. Could it all come back again? she wondered. She stroked her pearls.

She put her hand out to the mirror. She lightly traced the outline of her face with her finger. But the mirror was a wall between herself and the warm flesh behind it. She could not feel the contours of her face: the nose marked no rise, the lips no difference in texture. And it was cold. Her finger still on the mirror, it came to her that that was an apt metaphor for her relationship with him. She could see him, sense his contours and his warmth, but whenever she made a move to touch him, there would be a smooth, consistent surface. It was transparent, but it was unbreakable. At times she had felt he put it there on purpose and she had been furiously resentful. At others it had seemed that he was trapped behind it and was looking to her to set him free. She stood very still. Twice in the year she had lived in this flat she had locked herself in here: squeezing herself into the corner behind the door and crying till she could not breathe. Twice he had not come looking for her, and when she had finally crept out, exhausted, she had found him comfortable within his cloud of blue smoke in the living room, reading, with Bob Dylan on the record player. The bad times seemed to have been a succession of bathrooms. Hotel bathrooms all over the world had seen her locked in, head over the bowl, crying, or simply sitting on the tiled floor reading through the night while he slept alone, unknowing, in large double beds that mocked her.

She turned and walked back through the corridor to the living room. The cane-backed sofa and armchairs sat quietly in the dark. She crossed over to the sofa and sat down, feeling again the softness of the down-filled green-velvet-covered cushions. She examined them closely. The feathers were still escaping from the seams. Years ago, she had thought, In a couple of years all the feathers will have gone! But here she was, six years later, and they were still there and still escaping. She looked around. The books were all in place: economics and electronics to the left, art and literature to the right, and in the middle, history. The paperbacks were in the smaller bookcase built into the wall. On its lowest shelf were the records. There were far more albums there now than before. And the music center was new too. The old, battered record player had ended up with her. Together with a few of the old records.

She lifted her eyes to the wall above the music center. Her portrait had gone. Painted when she was twenty-one and given to them both as a wedding present. He had vowed he would always keep it, and when he had a study of his own he would hang it there. Now it hung in her parents' home, in her father's study. In its place was an old Syrian tapestry. It showed the Arab knight and poet Antar on horseback, and his beloved cousin Abla in a litter on a camel's back. Abla had been on a journey and Antar was proudly escorting her back to their settlement. His horse pranced, tail swishing and neck arched high, and Abla peeped coyly out to smile at him from behind the canopies of her litter. On one side were inscribed the verses:

> *And I remembered you*
> *When battle raged*
> *And as lance and scimitar*
> *Raced for my blood*
> *I longed to kiss*

> *Their glinting edges*
> *Shining like your smiling mouth*

and on the other:

> *I am the lord's knight*
> *Famed throughout the land*
> *For a sure hand with the lance*
> *And the Indian sword.*

They had bought it in Damascus. One day, wandering down the labyrinth of narrow streets that made up the covered market surrounding the Umaynad Mosque, they had come across a tiny shop selling fabrics and tapestries. They had gone in and spent time looking over the materials and she had spotted this one in black and gold. She had laughed as she showed it to him. "This could be your motto. He thought a lot of himself, like you." For a moment he had been defensive. Then he had trusted in her good faith and laughed and bought it.

Her remark had been true. He lived in heroic proportions and would have been better off as some medieval knight, be it Arab or Frank. He would have gone out and slain dragons and ghouls and rescued damsels in distress. He would have been kind to his squire and his horses and would have believed in the chastity of his wife weaving in her tower. And perhaps, in the Middle Ages, his belief would not have been misplaced.

Another memory sprang to her mind. "The Spartans," he was fond of saying, "spent the last day before Marathon adorning themselves and combing their hair. They knew they were going to die." On their last day, he had come up to the living room in the cottage. His car had been packed. He was setting off down the M-1. He was drunk. But he was very well dressed, with a velvet jacket and a silk foulard. "I have combed my hair," he had said quietly, swaying at the top of the stairs.

She pressed a hand to her head. Not again. Please. Not again. It's over now. Finished. Her eye caught her desk. It was cluttered with objects. She stood up and went over, looking at them absently. Papers, letters, ashtrays, an old half coconut shell, a silver flask in a leather case, some flying instruments salvaged from a wrecked plane, and a gun. She picked it up. An old Colt .45. "When you shoot yourself in the head," he had told her, "your brains splatter all over the place. It's a hell of a mess."

"What can you do?" she had asked.

"Put your head in a plastic bag first."

The doorbell rang. She stood very still. It rang again. She walked slowly to the door and opened it. A boy stood holding a carefully folded pile of shirts. He handed them to her. She took them automatically.

"How much?"

"Twelve shirts by five piastres is sixty piastres," he said.

She went back to the living room, put the shirts on the sofa, and took her purse from her handbag. She took out seventy piastres and went back to the door.

"Take these."

"Do you have anything else for ironing?"

"No thanks," she replied, "not today."

She closed the door and turned again to face the flat. The dining room was now directly opposite her. She walked over. These had been her favorite pieces of furniture. Solid dark oak in a rustic style with carved lions' heads for handles. The massive table and sideboards stood waiting for her in the gloom. She opened the small upright sideboard they had used as a bar. It was as well stocked as ever and the crystal goblets sparkled quietly inside. She put out her hand. She had treasured these goblets and the formal china with gold and green edging. She looked around. The table would be covered with the beige and gold damask tablecloth and the room lit by candles in silver candlesticks. Where is the silver? she wondered. The trays and candlesticks were not in their places on the sideboards. She started looking for them. She opened the sideboard doors and peered inside, and there were the delicate little blue and white Japanese bowls. Bought in Tokyo. A great tiredness overwhelmed her. She put out a hand behind her, dragged up a chair, and sat down. The whole world. What city was left that she could go to and not find memories? Why not give in? Why not come back? Tokyo. All those pretty little girls in red miniskirts and white cotton gloves operating the elevators and incessantly bowing: "Thank you for shopping at our store, we hope you have a good day, we hope you will come back." All those gaudy shrines, presided over by sleepy-eyed Buddhas who had sat inscrutable as she clapped her hands and tied a piece of paper with a wish to the sacred tree. She had always wished for one thing. Incoherently. Make it right. Dear God,

Buddha, Allah, make it right. She felt the pricking of tears behind her eyes, but she would not cry. Two whole years had passed since that day in the living room of the cottage and she was not going to cry anymore.

She resumed her search for the missing silver and in a corner of the larger sideboard she found it. She drew it out. Trays, ashtrays, candlesticks, and a trophy inscribed "Miss Cairo University 1970." Eight years ago . . . All were tarnished. Bits of them were quite black. Typical again, she thought. He can't bear to see them tarnished and can't be bothered to get them polished, so he tucks them away in a corner and hopes they'll disappear. Or maybe he even hopes that by some miracle when next he thinks to look, he'll find them gleaming and bright. She rubbed a corner of the cup with her thumb. I wonder if he has any polish? she thought again. With a surge of energy she made for the kitchen. She stood looking around. His mother had bought them the kitchen fittings and her aunt had made the curtains. So pretty, with their blue flowers and white broderie anglaise trimming. They were still there, the sunlight shining gently through them. And there was the breakfast bar and the little two-eyed cooker where she'd learned to make goulash soup. She looked at the sink. There were two unwashed glasses. She took off her rings and watch and started to wash them. They'd always had friends around. Parties. How had she managed with such a tiny kitchen? Such a tiny fridge? She opened the fridge. Even the containers had been carefully chosen and had blue flowers to match the curtains. In the door were two bottles of beer and a bottle of white wine and seven eggs. She opened a round container. It was full of jam. She dipped a finger in it and licked. Date jam. His mother's date jam. She had a vivid image of him: a serious little boy of seven, playing in the sea at Alexandria. His nanny wades out from the beach holding up her galabiya with one hand, the other holding out a sandwich. She waves and calls, "Come out now. Come and have a date jam sandwich!" When he was seven she had not yet been born, but the image was vivid in her mind from stories repeated by his mother every time she gave her a present of a large jar of date jam. She made it with her own two hands. The dates were laid neatly one on top of the other and in the center of each one was an almond and a clove. Then they were covered with syrup. "It always brought him out," she would say. "He loved the sea, but he loved his mother's date jam more." And she would laugh.

She put the lid back on the pot and closed the fridge door. Where were those photos of him as a child that she had had framed? They were not hanging anywhere. But then he had never been particularly keen on them. She remembered the silver. She rummaged around in the kitchen cupboards. She found some shoe polish and some powdered soap, but that was all. She closed the cupboard doors and went back to the dining room. Slowly she put the silver back into the corner of the sideboard. I could buy some, she thought. I could go right now and buy some polish and come back and do it. She closed the sideboard door and looked up at the wall above it. There they were. The framed maps of Sinai. The two old army maps he had used when he made his celebrated trek across the desert.

He had gone with a friend. They had traveled by jeep and by camel, spending days at the monastery of Saint Catherine and weeks with the Sinai Bedu. She had listened wide-eyed to his tales of that trip. "Can we do something like that together?" she had asked. "But I've already done it," he had said, laughing. And it was true. He had already done it. He had already done a lot of things. His memories were more vivid to her than her own. She had no memories. She had had no time to acquire a past, and in her worst moments, locked up in some bathroom, it had seemed to her that his past was devouring the present.

She pulled herself away from the deserts and mountains and turned to the living room. Her eyes fell on the pile of fresh shirts on the couch. She crossed over and picked them up carefully and walked automatically to the wardrobe in the corridor. She pulled open the left-hand door, and sure enough, there were the shelves of clean ironed shirts. She put away the ones she was carrying. The whites with the whites and the coloreds with the coloreds, noting as she did so how many were unfamiliar to her. Then, on an impulse, she pulled open the right-hand door. Suits and jackets hung quietly in place. At the end of the row was a fur-lined overcoat they'd bought at Harrods. "Your fur," she used to call it. "Who's sitting warm inside his fur?" And he'd always grin and pull the collar up around his neck. She put out her hand and stroked it, then started to pull it out. Behind it, something hung shrouded in a white sheet. She left the coat and, taking hold of the other hanger, removed the shroud. She found herself looking at her wedding dress. It hung from her hand, a dream creation in white and gray lace, embroidered lovingly with tiny seed pearls. Her hand shaking, she hung it back in the cupboard and hung the sheet over it. She knelt down to adjust the sheet around the train and her fingers hit a smooth object. She pulled it out. A white cardboard box. She knew what it was. Hesitantly she opened the lid, and sprang up and back with a scream. Her veil and small, pearl-embroidered Juliet's cap nestled in tissue paper. They were covered with black moths. Trembling and with cold hands, she put the lid back on the box and carried it to the kitchen. She put it in the sink, searched for the matches, and set fire to it. She stood and watched it burn; then she cleared up the ashes and washed the sink and her hands. Her stomach turned again, and again she rushed to the bathroom. Always bathrooms. She flushed the toilet and rinsed out her mouth, then slowly made her way to the bedroom. She pulled herself up onto the large four-poster bed and lay there, careful to keep her sandaled feet off the fine pink linen sheets. She lay still as the world pitched and tilted and, weakened now, she felt the tears creep sideways from her eyes onto the bed. This too was familiar. Lying there dizzy, weeping, sick. Recurring illnesses that they said were hysterical. "What's wrong with you?" they asked. "Why don't you settle?" She didn't know, she always said. She *didn't* know. She lay on the bed and sobbed herself to sleep, carefully keeping her feet over the edge.

The instant she woke she saw the velvet-papered walls and the white lace curtains. She did not have an instant's doubt about where she was. She knew. What she did not know was *when* she was. What happened? she asked, lying on the bed.

Where is he? What did I dream? She lifted herself up on one elbow and saw her reflection in the dressing-table mirror. She did not see a round-faced girl with long, straight black hair. Instead she saw, with recognition, relief, and sorrow, the woman with the curly hair and the pearl necklace. She lowered herself gently off the bed, straightened the linen, and left the room.

She went to the living room and headed for the right-hand side of the large bookcase. She scanned the literature shelves and picked out five books on seventeenth-century poetry. Then, carrying the books, she picked up her handbag. She walked through the flat and out of the door. She switched off the light and pulled the door to. Then she put her key in the lock and turned it firmly, twice.

Out in the sun, she got into her little red car. She put the five books and her handbag on the passenger seat and drove down the west side of the square. She maneuvered carefully around the potholes till she came out of the bumpy road and to the roundabout once again. There she picked up speed.

Mandy

Wednesday, 28 December 1978

Dear Mummy,

I am writing to you from New York—although by the time you get this I'll be back in London. We're visiting (or "visiting with," as they all say) some friends of Gerald's. He had his heart set on coming here for the New Year, so here we are. This is our third day and I haven't really seen anything of the city yet, but I will soon.

I saw Saif in London just before I left and he seems okay. I found I envied him his pretty flat dreadfully. This trip has put off my accommodation problem for a bit, but I think Gerald and I are beyond working things out (did you know all along?) and I'm going to try and find a place of my own as soon as I get back to London. Although there is something quite bracing about having all my possessions in the car and being "of no fixed address."

Gerald doesn't think so at all, of course. He's ravenous for the three-bedroom house—preferably in the Boltons—and the garageful of Porsches. Maybe he'll get them someday; I wish him luck, but I'm truly fed up with him being angry with me for "having once had them."

Anyway, Saif has got himself a lean-looking one too. Female, of course. And American. Yes, I'm afraid the days of Lady Caroline of the tiger-shooting, coolie-whipping father are over, and the chances of her riding for the Gezira Club as plain Mrs. Madi have quite disappeared. He brought this new one also up to the north of England in my last fortnight, when I was printing out the thesis. He was taking her on the Windermere round. To a little hotel run by two gay chaps where we once had dinner. He was taking her there for a couple of days and phoned me and asked could he come up and borrow the Lancia? And I said I'd rather he took it because I was going to be finishing soon and how was I going to drive two cars away from that place? So they came up on the train and I met them. I paid twopence and went down to platform 3 as I had done so many times before and the train came in and he stepped out as he had done so many times before. As usual, he was a bit shorter than I remembered, and as usual, I wasn't quite sure what I was doing there. Then she stepped out after him and solved my problems. She was dressed up like a Lichfield ad. A Country Casual outfit that he'd wanted me to buy back in '75: a just-below-the-knee camel skirt, a russet cashmere jumper, and a cape—would you believe?—with a Burberry check scarf, brown

Mandy

*Charles Jourdan boots, and an Etienne Aigner handbag to match.
She even had fawn gloves. She looked terribly lost inside all that. It
didn't suit her at all. Anyone could see he had only just bought it for
her. Her name is Mandy. She's the small-boned wiry New York type.
Arty-looking, with frizzed-out brown hair, an amazingly clear, lit-
up kind of skin, and a very slight cast in her left eye, which is actually
quite appealing.*

*Anyway, seeing her in those clothes was weird. They're just the
kind of thing he's always thought elegant women should wear, and
I'm sure she would never, ever have chosen them for herself. Do you
remember that scene I told you about in Harvey Nichols where he
stopped in front of a mannequin and said, "That would look good on
you," and I started to cry and kept asking, "Why does it always have
to be beige?" Well, seeing this freewheelin', verse-writin' (he says
she is a poet and a photographer—both!), dope-smokin' (you mustn't
be shocked, Mummy, everybody does it here. And you mustn't worry:
I'm not doing it) New Yorker dressed like English country brought
that side of it all back to me, and I was so relieved to be through and
out. But I must admit I felt a pang of jealousy: it was the idea of him
looking after her, I guess. Like seeing you or Daddy being really nice
to someone other than me! I mean, I wasn't jealous jealous: I didn't
want to swap places with her or anything, and I certainly didn't
wish her any harm. I felt sorry for her: she looked so out of place, so
uneasy, and so determined. I suppose it must be rough being dragged
off to meet "the wife," even an estranged wife, as he once put it (neither of us has mentioned a divorce yet).*

*Anyway, he was looking great: better than any time since we got
engaged. He's stopped trying not to smoke and is back to forty cigarettes*

a day, except it's Freiburg and Tryer now, not Rothmans. He's terribly chic and he's in a bearded phase. He looks like a gentleman sea captain. We all shook hands and smiled and I asked about the journey and we said they'd picked a lovely day for it. Then I took them to the best that the town had to offer in the way of cafés, a large room full of senior citizens and irate young mothers. It all smelled of frying, and they in their Bond Street outfits looked like posh relatives come to give a poor student a treat.

So we had tea and I felt terribly like some mother being shown her son's new girl, and like a mother I thought, She's not good enough for him, which she isn't. She isn't pretty enough and she doesn't have that unwavering serenity he needs. She probably is in love with him; it's hard not to be. But also I think she's edgy and restless and won't be happy with him and won't make him happy. I also fear there must be some gold-digging element there because she's so obviously on the make and he looks prosperous. I don't think his money can possibly last very long, though. A year maximum—and I don't know what he'll do then.

Well, they drove off to the Lakes, a battery of cameras on the backseat and all that. And he phoned to say the hotel was every bit as lovely as we had thought it was when we had dinner there with Mario two and a half years ago. Three days later he came back alone to say good-bye. He said he'd left her in town to do some shopping, but who on earth was going to shop in a little town in the north when they could shop in London in a couple of hours? She just didn't want to go through the meeting-the-wife routine again and I don't blame her.

✧ ✧ ✧ ✧

Mandy

She met us at the station and she was so friendly I could
have thrown up. Eastern inscrutableness, I guess. Her
name is Asya. It actually means Asia in Arabic. *He* says it
can also mean "the cruel one" and "she who is full of
sorrow." She insisted on taking us for tea at this dump
that reeked of stale frying oil—except of course neither
of them would know what that was. They must have
thought it was quaint and picturesque because it was
down a dirty, cobbled lane backing onto the marketplace. Everybody else there was either some bearded old
woman out for her week's supply of cheap cabbages or
a harassed young mom with overloaded baskets and
stroller. People that couldn't go anywhere better. It was
a depressing scene. (It was like a parable, actually: youth
on its way through a lousy life to old age. It makes me
wonder why we all bother to go on.)

We sat there picking at some greasy pastry and drinking overboiled tea and making dumb conversation:

> She: It's quite a long trip up from London really, is
> it not?
> Me: You must have made it lots of times?
> She: At least twenty, I should think.

That kind of thing.

Except then they got started on Sadat's Jerusalem
trip and couldn't stop. Well, finally she asks for the bill,

and holding it between two slim brown fingers, she raises her eyebrows with just the hint of a smile (very charmingly done): "This is hardly worth fighting over, is it?"

She left what must have been a 50 percent tip and handed over the car keys on—natch—a solid gold key ring.

"It's really beautiful up in Windermere. I'm sure you'll have a lovely time."

She didn't quite say "children," but she easily could have. And of course she was careful not to mention the name of the hotel or let on if she'd been up here with him.

"If you would just drop me off at the house?"

But he wanted to stop by his college first.

He says she's finishing a dissertation, getting a Ph.D. Only the way he says it, you're not sure if it's a joke or what. (I'm trying to be completely fair here. I'm always 100 percent honest in my journal—otherwise what's the point of keeping it?) She is good-looking; not a stunner or anything, but okay, with a lot of shiny black hair with a loose wave in it. I think she's older than me, but I couldn't tell her precise age; I never can with Eastern people.

Once we get to the college he wants to go for a walk. All it is, is a small-town campus, and we keep bumping into people who know him and all he says is "This is Mandy" and they nod and smile politely and don't say "Mandy who?" I'm getting pretty fed up by then: this was billed as a trip to the Lake District, not down memory lane. I don't say anything, though, because if I've learned anything by now, it's that he moves at his own pace and does what he wants and screw the rest of the world. And if the world objects or has something different in mind, why then, screwing it is just that much more fun. So I trail around after him and smile and say "Uh-huh?" and "Hi" and get madder and madder.

Then I get to thinking he wouldn't be taking me around this place if he was planning on splitting soon, would he? And so I'm not mad anymore. I can't really afford to be mad at him anyway. For one thing, he's paying for this suite. (I've never stayed in a suite before. It's great. Like, now I can't sleep, but I don't have to lie next to him in the dark or camp out in the bathroom: I can sit out here in this very beautiful "olde English" room with the fire gently dying in the grate—this is really a room to write poems in. But I must carry on with this because I haven't been getting much chance lately. Also I feel that this is IMPORTANT and I want to always remember how it felt.)

He's paying for this trip. He pays for everything. Ever since I met him three weeks ago, I've never once had to use my own money. Which is just as well, since all I've got is my ticket home and five hundred-dollar traveler's checks stashed away—what's left of two years

I THINK OF YOU

of saving. Except not all that five hundred dollars is really mine. There is:

$14   Owed to Clark for one week's rent when I moved out so fast. Unless he managed to sublease the room right away.

$50   Borrowed from Jackie in Paris—to be collected when she comes over.

$20   Acid in Amsterdam (alliteration!)—for Don when he comes over.

So that really leaves me with $416 that I can honestly call my own. Wow! That wouldn't last two days the way we're going. He must have stashes and stashes of dough, the way he throws it around. He thinks what you do when you run out of clean socks is go down to Harrods and buy another two dozen pairs. (The reason he runs out of socks is he changes three times a day. I used to think Arabs weren't very particular about all that, but this guy is paranoid with showers and clean clothes. Also, all his socks are black!) All this shopping suits me fine. He's always bought me something too. Like the outfit I was wearing this morning. I was right to wear it because it's called a lady's traveling outfit, and that's what I was doing—traveling. I saw her clocking it, right there in the station. I guess it looks kind of new: the creases sharp and the nap all going in one direction and all that. She probably knows the sort of thing he'd buy as well. You're not married to someone for six years without knowing that. Not that you'd think it from the jeans and sweater she was wearing. But then she doesn't need to bother anymore. He doesn't mind spending his money on me. He does it like it was the most natural thing in the world. Maybe that's Eastern too: women being chattels and all that. (Does *chattel* have anything to do with cattle? Maybe, because the possessions of nomadic peoples would probably be livestock.) I wonder how much of that I really can put up with? It's fun so far, but it's only been three weeks. She must have gotten fed up with it, though—and she was born to it.

Why the hell do I have to keep on thinking about her? I wonder how much *he* thinks about her? A lot, I'd guess, although he'd never admit it. Admit it? He'd never discuss it even. He'll maybe answer a straight question, but not always.

But seeing him with her today was really something: he was like some kid showing off. Showing off to his mom. And playing her up. One minute he'd be all intimate half-smiles and the next he'd be needling her. And she was all serene and beautiful, taking it all. It's sick if you ask me. Sick. It could have been beautiful: two people—having passed through the Storm That Made Their Marriage and then the Storm That Wrecked It—left with a Deep and Intimate Friendship. But in their case it's just sick. I don't know why.

Wow! I got upset just then.

Man, I'd go crazy without this journal. I had a smoke and a small Scotch and here I am again. I put everything in here: accounts, observations, fragments, poems (must remember to copy out two written on the Amsterdam–London train), even the days I get my period and the nights I make love.

Talking of making love, I just went and looked at him as he lay sleeping. He looks so peaceful when he sleeps. Not everyone does. Clark ground his teeth all night. But Saif just turns on his side and curls up like a baby. I've laid for hours staring at his back: the color of light caramel candy. Sometimes I'd like to lick it, but I don't know what he'd think of that. He's into some kind of Eastern thing he says is called Carezza: it involves him doing things to me very slowly (nothing weird or far-out, just stroking and things) and me doing nothing at all. It's not a problem since I orgasm at least once each time, but I don't always see what's in it for him.

He's very cute, though, as well as being rich. Once or twice he's acted strange—all gloomy and smoky and wouldn't speak at all—but mostly he's fun to be with, except I don't always know if he's joking or what. He won't ever talk—I mean, really TALK—about anything personal, but I guess it takes time to build up communication.

What I'd like to do now is take a photo of him sleeping. The flash would wake him, though, and I haven't got my tripod and his kit is down in the car. I'll take lots of shots of him tomorrow. Maybe I'll take a shot of him taking a shot of me. No, that should be a third person really, to make the point: a third person taking a photo of two people, hiding behind their cameras, shooting each other, with the trees and fallen leaves all around them and the lake in the background. It's so beautiful up here. We've just caught the trees before they shed the last of their leaves.

Well, I guess we'll have a nice day tomorrow. I don't know if he will want to go on the lake, but we'll drive around it and he said there was a neat place in William Wordsworth's hometown where we could have tea— that means tea and cakes here. I ought to go to bed if I'm going to be in any kind of shape in the morning. But I'm not sleepy. What I'd really like right now is a joint, but I'm fresh out. Okay, what I'll do is, I'll copy out these two poems now, then go to bed.

I

A Russian dissident sits across from me in the park.
He must be a dissident because
he's Russian, and he's
here
in New York City.
Does he know that Central Park
is

muggers only
after dark?

A woman with a toddler walks past
if you can call it
walking:
that motherbaby dance.
Right and left he staggers
leading
distracted
only going forward diagonally
by chance.

Soon I'll pack my camera
my notebook
my ballpoint pen
and come home to
where
she still combs her hair
for you.

You dig, you say, my fishnet tights
my jaunty ass
my cigarette
but now I sit and wonder
do wives wear fishnet tights—in Russia?

I've cheated a bit here because I've worked on the
poem before copying it out. I only had the first two

sections and the ending was different. But I think it's a lot better like this.

It really is strange how poems work. On an Amsterdam boat train I remember Central Park and I start a poem. A month later, I add in something from today and—wow! It's there.

I think I have something good here. When we go back to London I'll type it up and start a folder so I can show it to him. This journal stays locked. I don't do poem number two now. I go to bed.

◇ ◇ ◇ ◇

Sunday, 12 March 1979

Dearest Mummy,

Thank you thank you thank you for your letter and for everything in it. Can I be independent and have—at the same time—a guardian angel? You'll be glad to know—will you be glad to know?—that everything is moving pretty fast. I've actually started at Citadel Publishing, although we haven't really agreed on a salary yet (Vivien tells me I should hold out for more than they're offering) and I've used your money—as you said—to make a down payment on a little flat in Kensington. It's terribly sweet—or will be when it's ready. I'm supposed to move into it next month. Meanwhile—you'll never guess—I'm borrowing Saif's flat while he's away. It feels really odd being in his atmosphere again like this. He's in the States. I don't really know what he's doing there—except he's taken Mandy (I told

*you about her visit up north) with him. He could be meeting her folks
or he could be getting rid of her. I don't know—he gave me a portfolio of her oeuvre a while back—*

Asya pauses and looks up from her typewriter. Maybe that's
not fair. After all, Mandy was—presumably—doing her best.
And she probably didn't ask Saif to give it to her. Maybe she
was horrified at the idea. No, if she'd been horrified, it
wouldn't have happened. Saif would hardly have pressed her.
Asya can just see them: Mandy going on about it—about the
possibility of getting it published, Saif finally saying, "I can
give it to Asya if you like; she's in publishing."

"But what am I supposed to do with this?" Asya had asked.

"I haven't the foggiest," Saif said.

"I mean, I'm not—well, you *know* Citadel isn't that kind
of publisher. They do schoolbooks."

"Send her a nice rejection slip," he said. "That'd be
something."

Asya picks up Mandy's portfolio—again. Had he particularly wanted her to see this? Was there a message in here
somewhere?

A set of photographs of buildings with mirrored windows, and on the facing page:

> *We see what
> we want
> to see.
> You*

Mandy

see
your own
reflection.

A set of photographs of trees—autumnal—and a blurred figure, Saif surely, vanishing into the distance, and on the facing
page:

Next year
once again they
will flower.
You
will not
return.

Asya sits back in her chair. Is this meant for her? But it was
Mandy who wrote it, not Saif. Does this mean that whatever
had been written she still would have turned it into a personal
message? She gazes out the dark window. Last month she had
stood out there, under that tree she can now make out as only
a dark shadow on the other side of the road, and she had
watched him. She had watched him and known that she
could not go back, sit companionably in the other armchair,
and reach for a magazine. She leans sideways trying to see the
sky, to see if there are any stars. Imagine the world out there,
full of signals. You pick one up and it seems to speak to you.
To you alone. Is this how horoscopes work? If she were to ask

him . . . Asya has to smile; it's exactly the type of question he hates. And yet he sends her this—this portfolio.

She turns back to the table. Gerald would like it. Gerald would *love* it. It's just his kind of thing. Multimedia too. She flicks through the pages and comes again to the longest of the poems and stops, as before, at the last verse. "So," she says out loud, "she can say *ass*. Well, big deal. Anyone can say *ass*. I can say it. Ass. Jaunty ass. Big deal." She turns back to her type-writer.

—and they're vaguely okay, I suppose. Not my kind of thing. Anyway, Mummy darling, you're going to have to come over next summer—

Satan

"I don't understand anything. Are you both joking or what? Do you think I've gone senile that I can't get a straight answer from either of you? So my son is crazy; he's got an armored head. I know that, but I know also that he treasures you like the light of his eyes and he could never do without you. Yes, I know there's a woman: some low creature has pulled him for two or three weeks; absence does terrible things, child, and it was you who chose to put countries between you. I'm not making excuses for him. Don't ever think that. I am *furious* with him. I've *told* him and I've *sworn*: after this time I'll not enter a home of his until things are all right between you. I'll not enter any home of his unless you are its mistress."

"Tante," Asya says when she can edge a word in. "Tante, It's not like that. What's happened between Saif and me is nothing at all to do with Clara."

"Clara! And you can put her name on your tongue? Your nerves, my dear, your nerves!" Adila Hanim's voice pitches a couple of notes higher. "I tell you, I didn't even believe him when he told me you knew." She reaches for a casserole dish on a high shelf, and before her daughter-in-law can move to help her, she has banged it down on the cooker. "She actually has the boldness to come here with him. What does she think? She imagines I'm going to welcome her? That we're all going to sit down together and talk about this and that? I wouldn't even shake her hand!"

Asya stands in the doorway of the kitchen, her arms folded behind her. "Well, you must have annoyed him then," she says gently.

"Let him be annoyed. It's time someone annoyed him. Staying with her in a hotel, openly, when he knows I'm coming."

Beyond her mother-in-law's solid figure, a tall narrow window stands ajar. Visible beyond it are daylight and a brick wall. But Asya knows that it opens onto the narrow passage between the two Victorian houses. To the right is the fence enclosing the gardens; to the left is the street.

"But, Tante, she was living with him here. He went to a hotel because he left the flat for you. It was natural that he should take her with him."

"Asya! Are you trying to give me a stroke?" Adila Hanim pauses with her hands on the rim of the pot into which she has just thrown a knob of butter. She stares reproachfully at her daughter-in-law. Why is Asya defending him? Like this, she, Adila, finds herself attacking Saif more and more; as though the matter gnawed at his mother's heart more than at his wife's. She looks at Asya, who tries to manage a small smile. Asya has changed. In the five years since they last met, she has changed. When she first came in and they hugged each other, then drew away with moist eyes, Adila had thought her daughter-in-law was still the same. But now she sees the changes. The black hair keeping more of its wave than it had ever been allowed in Cairo; the skin paler; the face newly defined, as though it had been sculpted out of its old childish roundness. But above all, the detachment, the holding back, to be seen in the eyes and in every stance of that slim body. Oh, child, child, whatever has happened to you? Adila Hanim turns away. "He could have stayed with me," she says.

"With you, Tante, yes. But with you and Hussein and Mira and her mother? There's only one bedroom here. I can't think how you're managing."

"Look, my dear"—Adila Hanim sighs as she starts chopping an onion into a bowl—"I didn't want them to come. I've been hearing for a while that there are problems between you two, so I thought I'd come over to try and mend things. Then Hussein, God preserve him, says 'Mama, I won't let you go alone; I'm coming with you.' The next thing I know his wife is coming too, because she might as well shop for the baby, and then Souma Hanim decides to come and help her daughter with the shopping. So here we are. And the place is tight; I mean, the rooms are nice and big, but there's only two of them, so we're all in each other's throats all the time. I know it's only for a few days, but I'm not used to this, child, I'm not used to this." She shakes her head sadly and bangs her knife against the edge of the bowl to shake off the last of the diced onion.

Asya presses back against the wall. She has not seen Tante Adila for five years, and although the brown hair still bravely holds its color, the face is more troubled and lined than she remembers. She must feel her daughter-in-law's newfound hardness. She must be hurt by it. But Asya isn't hard, not really. She longs to go over and put her arms around those solid shoulders and . . . and then what? Then they'd sit down and cry together. And in the end Asya still would not be able to give her mother-in-law the thing she wants most, the thing she's come all the way to London for. She watches as Adila Hanim turns on the tap.

On a corner of the ornately tiled floor, a small black kitten is chasing his tail. He is obviously having a lot of fun. Autotelic fun, thinks Asya; all he needs is his own tail—which is fortunate, since his own tail is all he's got. She's seen him before: he'd been around when she came here eleven days ago to give Saif some of the mail that kept arriving for him at her address. For a few minutes of her visit the kitten had been a small black ball of fur on her husband's immaculate white shoulder. Clara, he told her, his latest friend, had found this kitten and adopted him. She had named him Satan and spent hours looking after him. He'd also said that Clara would have loved to meet her but had gone out. She was Scots, he said, and spoke with *och* and *wee*. Her photo on the desk showed a dreamy, creamy oval face and a tumbling mass of auburn hair.

"What was I saying? Yes, I did not speak to her at all," Adila Hanim repeats. "I had to offer her tea, of course, because after all, this counts as my home while I'm here and she was in it. But apart from that I pretended not to even see her."

"It's not her fault, Tante," Asya begins weakly.

"Why are you defending her?" Adila Hanim shakes the water from her hands, wipes them on the front of her apron, and puts them on her waist as she turns around to face her daughter-in-law. Asya looks down at her shoes, a plain deep green, away from the sadness and puzzlement on the care-worn face.

"Explain it to me," Adila Hanim says. "I tell you, I just don't understand anymore."

"Well, what I mean is"—Asya shifts against the wall—"she isn't the first. There were others before her, and there are going to be others after her. She's just not terribly important—and anyhow, we had already left each other."

"Left each other! Spit from your mouth, child. It's just a little quarrel and it will pass. He'll get rid of the redheaded tart."

"She's not a tart." Asya realizes how odd she must sound. Either mad or phony. "What I mean is," she goes on, "it's sort of normal here. I mean, she met him and he was a single man—separated. I think she's in love with him. She probably thinks he's going to marry her."

"Marry her! He'll have to kill me first. Marry a daughter of a . . . a woman who'd take a respectable man off his wife? Living abroad has addled your brains, child. That's what's happened."

Adila Hanim peels potatoes in silence. The kitten flicks its tail, pounces at it, and loses it. Asya watches. She had offered to help but had been waved away. Should she insist? Should she be here at all? She knows the conversation isn't going the way Tante Adila wants it to, but then it never could have. Can she stand here and say she'd been unhappy for years? Say she's "known" another man but has left him? Say she loves Saif but has to be free?

When he'd phoned her to say that his mother was in London and wanted to see her, they had both known that Adila Hanim was here to try and put an end to the separation between them.

"If you don't want to go, that's fine. I'll tell her," Saif offered.

"No, I'll go. I ought to, and I'd like to see Tante."

"I'm not going," he said. "She'll have dinner laid out and it'll be hellish."

So here she is. She had known she'd have to stall on any intimate conversation. Yet she really loves Tante Adila and has missed her—misses her even more now that she's here. Maybe she had hoped somehow to make her feel not too bad about the whole thing. Well, this was a far cry from the days shared in the Madis' kitchen at home. The French windows open onto the garden where the three cats snoozed under the pear tree. Dada Nour preparing the vegetables, her daughter at the sink washing chopping boards, mixing bowls, graters as they were finished with. Tante and her at the table. Tante cooking, showing her how to rub the boiled pasta with raw egg before covering it with the sauce bolognese, how to recognize the exact moment when the pepper sizzling in the butter was ready for the rice. Tante hadn't thought *she* was a tart for visiting her son, for spending days in their home without her own parents knowing, for vanishing into his room for the afternoon.

"If you love my son," she once said to her, "you are loved by me." What would she say now if she knew the truth? Should she tell her the truth? She looks at her mother-in-law's grieving, betrayed face. What is the truth but every detail of the last nine years? How can it be told? And would it really make this easier? And anyway, shouldn't it be up to him? This is his family. Let them believe what he chooses for them to believe. Maybe he prefers the cad's role to that of the injured husband. She looks down at the kitten, busy now with a stray pistachio nut. Poor Clara. Bad luck to be the one around when this family disciplinary expedition showed up.

A little while ago it would have been Mandy. And before that, Lady Caroline. But it was just this gentle, tragic-faced girl's luck. Clara's medieval features made Asya think of the Lady of Shallott. True, she had only seen her photo—but she felt as if she knew her. She knows, for instance, that Clara is dreaming of a home in the shadow of the pyramids, of "bonny wee bairns" with brown skin and green eyes. She also knows for a certainty that within two months she'll be back in St. Andrews—possibly with a black cat.

Adila Hanim turns and catches Asya staring at the kitten. "Imagine. She's got a special comb for that cat. A special comb!" She snorts, then shakes her head and goes back to chopping the potatoes into the almost-ready chicken casserole.

When Asya arrived, Adila Hanim had been sharing the kitchen with her second son's mother-in-law, Souma Hanim. Each woman was determined that she would be the one to do all the cooking, the cleaning, and the washing-up. Adila Hanim—whose mother had died when she was five, leaving her a father and an older brother to look after—because she had never been and never could be in a house run by another woman. Souma Hanim, because she was well bred to an extreme and would never allow it to be said of her that she had sat around and let her daughter's mother-in-law slave over the sink and the stove. So the two women, trying to work in this cupboard calling itself a kitchen—a fraction of the size of the rooms they were accustomed to—had been bumping into each other, reaching across each other, easing past each other, urging each other to go for a walk with your son/daughter on this beautiful June day; to go and rest in the living room and I'll make some tea because there's only one apron, one carving knife, one grater, and anyway, everything's almost ready.

Asya's arrival broke the deadlock. It was obvious her mother-in-law would wish for a word with her in private, and since Hussein was in the living room and Mira was in the bedroom, it was now possible for Souma Hanim to retire with grace and tact and go check on her pregnant daughter.

"Anyway," Adila Hanim says, putting the lid firmly on the simmering casserole and grinding pepper into the butter heating for the rice, "I'm going to give him a few words when he gets here today. And Hussein intends to speak to him too. It's true Hussein's only his younger brother, but circumstances force our hand."

"He might not be coming, Tante, you know—"

"He's coming, dear. I've told him."

Mira appears in the kitchen doorway. Mira is seven months married and five months pregnant, and this, she feels, gives her an advantage over her senior sister-in-law, who has been married for five years and has only a miscarriage to her name. Her importance had become evident to her not so much when she first learned she was pregnant or when her tummy began to swell and her breasts to grow tender, but when she felt the baby kick inside her. She knew then that she was in possession of an immense and secret power. When she lay in bed that night and the baby celebrated the freedom afforded to it by this position, she reached for her husband's hand and placed it—to his delight and wonder—on her gently thumping belly. At that moment, as far as she was concerned, he relinquished his priority position in the household: baby came first; she, the bearer, came second; and her husband came last. No wonder, then, that she who used to jump up so eagerly could now sit back and let her mother-in-law remove her empty glass of tea, take it to the kitchen and wash it. No wonder that she could sit placidly, hand on stomach, vaguely aware of her husband fixing his own supper tray in the kitchen. And no wonder again that—feeling she had the sacred words, the unanswerable argument that would right all wrongs between her husband's brother and his wife—she should touch her sister-in-law's hand, saying "I want to talk to you," and precede her into the bedroom.

Asya is surprised because she and Mira met only an hour ago and she cannot imagine that this newcomer thinks she has anything to contribute to this already crowded situation. She glances at her mother-in-law, but Tante Adila is busy with the rice and trying to look as though it were an everyday happening for her two daughters-in-law to engage in girlish tête-à-têtes. Asya follows Mira into the bedroom and pushes the door to. Both women sit on the edge of the bed. There is nowhere else to sit.

Mira's eyes follow her own finger as it traces the ridges on the purple candlewick bedspread. Asya folds her hands on her knees and waits. She has not particularly taken to Hussein's wife. One would think Hussein could have done better for himself than this puffy, solemn girl. He is very good-looking— maybe the handsomest of the three Madi brothers—and knows it; he always wears a gold chain around his neck and his mustache trimmed just so, and he'd always been big with the girls at the club and at college. How odd, after all the jokes they'd shared, all the football matches they'd cheered together in the large, cool living room of his parents' house, after the firelit dinners, the camp beds she'd fixed him in the north of this country, how odd that he should now be sitting out there, in his brother's rented living room, with a newspaper, like a stranger. He had not spoken except to greet her and had merely shaken her hand politely when he opened the door. She sensed his puzzlement and also his disapproval. Come to think of it though, they'd never actually had any *real* conversations, and whenever he'd expressed an opinion—which he didn't often do—it had always been more restrained, more ordinary, than she'd expected. Also, as far as she knew, he had never ever brought a girl home. She would not have lacked a welcome, for—although Asya distinctly got the feeling that Mira did not get along well with her mother-in-law—Tante Adila was the most openhearted and hospitable of women, reserving her small store of animosity exclusively for Tante Durriya, the wife of her adored older brother. Maybe Hussein deserves his ponderous, silent, doubtless well-dowried bride, she thinks.

Across the room, by the French windows, unopenable onto the back patio, a dark patch begins to unfold itself on the carpet. It straightens onto four frail legs, steps into a medallion of pale sunshine, and stretches itself thoroughly. Then it rolls over onto its back and scrambles again to its feet. Its nose, ears, bright yellow eyes, and tail are all quivering with alert curiosity.

"Ah. So that's where you've been."

Asya bends and scratches her fingernails on the carpet. The kitten is upon them instantly. There they play, the hand and the cat—scratching, advancing, poking, pouncing, retreating—until Mira, stung by this unseemly display of frivolity, straightens up, captures her own wandering hand, rolls it into a fist, coughs slightly, and says, "There are problems between you and Saif?"

Asya glances up.

"Oh, no. It's all over. There aren't any problems anymore."

"But I heard . . . I heard that you're going to leave him."

The kitten is on its back, paws raised, waiting to strike at Asya's hovering hand. Even its belly is jet black.

"We've already left each other—almost a year ago."

Asya, tired of bending, scoops Satan onto her knee. He weighs nothing at all.

"But everybody says you love him," Mira says.

"I do love him," Asya patiently repeats, "but not to be married to him."

Mira's voice is impatient. "What do you mean?"

Asya looks at the warm black fur on her knee. She strokes its panting side with her thumbs and can feel the kitten purring. Who is this woman sitting here questioning her? Then she considers that living at home in the heart of the family, while all this trouble was brewing abroad, Mira must have heard her—Asya—discussed a thousand times. She very probably imagines that she does know her, that they are indeed sisters-in-law. Yet how can she truly explain anything to her?

She sighs. "I mean that I love him very, very much, but that over the last few years we've grown apart and I don't think we love each other in the way married people should. One loves people in different ways—"

She pauses, and Mira cuts in: "Asya, you're twenty-nine, aren't you?"

Asya glances at her. "Yes," she says.

And now Mira draws out her indisputable, unanswerable ace. She considers it, then leans forward and places it gently on the candlewick bedspread. "Don't you want to have a baby with him?"

Asya shakes her head slowly, stroking the kitten. "No," she says.

"No? How do you mean, no?"

"No," says Asya. "No, I don't."

After that, there is nothing to be said. But to get up and go would mean that offense had been taken, and besides there is nowhere to go except the living room, where Hussein sits rustling the *Evening Standard,* or the tiny kitchen, where the mothers-in-law are clanking the pots. So Mira folds her hands over her belly and lies back, duty done. Asya is clearly beyond reach and is probably even going with someone as she had heard said, although Tante Adila always denies it and springs to her first daughter-in-law's defense. But then, Tante Adila is willing to be a fool where Saif and his wife are concerned.

And why am I so sure? Asya wonders, stroking the kitten. Am I really so sure, so completely sure that I don't want his baby? And in her mind once again, the image forms: there he is, the child she had imagined as she lay on the sofa all those years ago, willing him to hold on, to stay in the womb. He is two years old, wearing soft, dark velvet pants and a white T-shirt, his face round and serious and dark-eyed, as in the photos of Saif as a baby. His bare, plump feet are planted sturdily on the wooden floor and he is occupied with something, some toy obscured from her by the arm of the chair he leans against. He would have been six years old now. *She hath miscarried of her savior,* they said of Anne Boleyn.

The kitten jumps off her knee and she stands up. No. She walks over to the sealed window and stands looking at the bare but sunlit patio. No. I am not going to start thinking about it all over again. No. It's over. It's really over and I know that it's over. The child is long gone, and the marriage is over, and Saif is all right now. He is over the worst of it. And he's started having girlfriends again. She can think of herself as an interlude in his life, a nine-year interlude. And she is not jealous of them. Not of one. Not Nicola or Jenny, both friends of hers and each taking great trouble that she should not know—as though they couldn't believe she didn't care. Not of Lady Caroline or Mandy or this Scots girl with the creamy skin and the thigh-length hair—Clara, who adopts stray kittens. Poor Clara, who is taking the brunt of Tante Adila's disappointment and displeasure.

The bedroom door is pushed open and Adila Hanim seethes in. The kitten streaks out.

"So he's not coming then or what?" Adila Hanim is wiping her hands roughly on a kitchen cloth. The lines from the corners of her nostrils around her mouth and into her chin are etched deep, and her chin has never looked so square and hard as it does now.

Asya feels sorry. So sorry. "But I told you, Tante."

"Told me what and didn't tell me what, Asya? Last night when I spoke to him he said yes."

"The word yes saves trouble. Saif always does that."

"So he's not coming?"

"I—I don't think so."

"All right. In any case, dinner's ready, so you two come and eat."

Out in the living room, the table in the wide bay window—the table where he has his Bohemian banquets of a joint of cold meat, ten cheeses, pickles, French bread, and red wine—is laid for six. Hussein is already sitting at what seems to have become his usual place: at his mother's left, facing the window. Souma Hanim is ladling out soup from a big white tureen at the center of the table.

Adila Hanim sets down a large basket of bread rolls, then sits down heavily at the other end of the table from where Souma Hanim is apparently about to sit. Asya moves to sit at her mother-in-law's right.

Mira emerges from the bedroom and takes her place between her husband and her mother. And both the chair and the dish to Asya's right remain empty.

Everyone mutters "Bismillah" and raises their spoons. After a few mouthfuls, Mira angles her spoon delicately into her dish and sits back. Her mother stops eating.

She leans over, staring at her daughter anxiously: "Mais, qu'est-ce que tu as, chérie?"

"Nothing, maman. I've had enough."

"But you've hardly had any of it!"

"I've had enough."

Souma Hanim lays her spoon down and reaches out to feel Mira's forehead. "You don't have a temperature or anything."

"Did I say I had a temperature?"

Tante Adila is rather noisily finishing the last spoonful of her soup. Hussein has laid his spoon down in his empty dish. Asya feels a soft touch on her ankle. She slips off one shoe and secretly strokes the kitten with her bare foot.

"Well, what's wrong with the soup? Your Tante Adila and I are spending this whole trip in the kitchen for you to take two mouthfuls and leave the rest?"

"Maman, I'm full. I'm full. Ouf."

Tante Souma changes tack. "Ah, chérie, take a couple more spoonfuls, darling, for my sake. C'est un bon potage, ça. Tu dois manger, chérie. Tu dois. Même pour le petit."

Tante Adila collects four empty dishes and goes to the kitchen. Hussein, who speaks no French, sits silently staring out of the window.

"Maman, I just don't want any more soup." Mira clenches her hands and her engagement solitaire glints. Souma Hanim gazes at her daughter.

A crash in the kitchen is followed by a loud and scolding invocation to the Preventer of disasters. Adila Hanim staggers in using two bunched-up kitchen towels to hold a steaming and obviously dangerously heavy casserole.

Hussein gets to his feet. "Shouldn't you have called me to carry that?"

His mother lets the casserole bang down onto the king-size Lady and Unicorn mat in the center of the table and—without answering—turns around and marches back into the kitchen.

He stands for a moment staring at the empty doorway, then with a slight shrug, sits down and resumes gazing past Asya and out of the window.

"Well then, tu va manger un peu de ce poulet au casserole?"

The rice is placed on the table and Adila Hanim sits down with a fresh stack of six plates in front of her. The struggle between the complaints rising within her and the necessity of saving face in front of these two strange women—her second son's wife and his mother-in-law—have compressed her lips into a hard, thin line.

She starts serving. But as she bangs the spoon against the side of the plate to shake off a few grains of rice, she starts to mutter. "All day long I'm cooking and he doesn't even bother to show up. Well, tell me. Say, 'I'm sorry, Mama, I won't be able to come.' Since when have I forced him? Can anyone force him? Ever? To do anything? Never in his life has it been possible for anyone to make Saif do anything except what he has already inside his own head."

Asya receives her plate with lowered eyes and murmurs her thanks. She sits, the creator of all this dislocation and misery, and nothing she can say can make anything any better. And leaving won't help either. She can't leave—at least not until she has finished all the food that Tante chooses to give her and sipped at a glass of mint tea. She has to get out soon, though, and she has to avoid any chance of another conversation with Tante. That will definitely happen if she insists (as she should, being the cause of their coming to this servantless country) on washing the dishes. Tante Adila will corner her in the tiny kitchen and then . . . and then Asya might break down and tell her everything. So she must just be rude and escape immediately after the tea. Oh, if only Saif were here, he would have stopped his mother at the door and taken the dish from her and scolded her, he'd have talked to Hussein and caught Asya's eye and grinned at the French remonstrances, he'd have held out scraps of food to the kitten, and Tante Adila would have been happy. Oh, if only . . .

Glancing up from her plate, Asya sees that Satan is in the middle of the table. Keeping his front paws at a safe distance from the hot bowl, he stretches his neck and takes elegantly pointed sniffs at the aroma of stewed chicken.

"Mange, chérie, mange," Souma Hanim whispers solicitously, patting Mira's drooping shoulder.

Hussein springs to his feet, his face dark. "God curse your father, why don't you stay away from us?" he shouts and, grabbing the kitten by the neck, hurls it against the far wall. Asya stands up.

On the floor, in the far corner, the kitten crouches, utterly still. Souma Hanim glances up at Hussein, then goes back to concentrating on her daughter, who appears not to have noticed anything. Tante Adila continues to dissect her chicken wing.

"What have you done?" Asya tries to keep her voice low. "You've broken him. You've broken his back."

Hussein sits down and puts his elbows squarely on the table. Asya runs around the table toward the kitten. She bends over, not daring to touch it in case it slumps broken in her hand. Slowly and shakily, Satan gets up. He stands on trembling legs, shakes himself; then with a jaunty little leap, he is out of the room. Asya collects her handbag.

"Where are you going, child? Come and finish your food."

"No. Thank you, Tante Adila, no. What has the kitten done that Hussein should throw him at the wall like that? That's shameful, taking it out on a kitten. What has he done? I'm going, Tante. I'm sorry."

Asya is close to tears. She drives round to Blake's Hotel. She asks for her husband at the desk and then paces while she waits. He comes down smiling, in a pale cream cotton shirt and a maroon cravat, with a question in his eyes. What is the question? Is it merely "Why are you here?" Or is it "Now that you have seen what you are doing to your Tante Adila, are you thinking of coming back?"

"Hi," she says. "Look, it's wrong to leave that kitten there. Tante doesn't like him and Hussein is treating him badly."

"The cat?" He looks blank. "It's only for a couple of days."

"In a couple of days he could be dead."

Saif smiles. "Hussein is going to murder a kitten?"

"He threw him across the room just now and practically broke his back. I don't think you should leave him there."

"I can't bring a kitten to a hotel. It's only a couple of days."

His voice has hardened in that way she knows so well. He is both bored and unyielding. She knows what he is thinking; he's thinking, Here's another attack of the dramatics, another of the theatrical fits. Well, he can think what he pleases; he's well out of it now, isn't he? She feels the tears rising to her eyes and knows that she has lost.

"Clara will be miserable if something happens to him," she says.

Saif reaches in his pocket and takes out a pack of Rothmans. "You're concerned for Clara?" he asks.

The tears spill from her eyes and Asya turns away. She'll take the kitten. She'll go back and pick him up and take him away. It isn't right to leave Satan with those people. It simply isn't right.

Chez Milou

Milou sits behind the cash desk. There is a gray-checked rug on her knees and on the rug sits Athène. Athène is a comfortable dachshund the color of expensive leather. She is sleek and plump, but there's no doubt that she is growing old; you can see it in her eyes. Occasionally she ventures onto the floor and pauses briefly amidst the feet of the waiters. But then Milou gets anxious and leans over to look and call for her, and Athène hurries back. She has to be helped onto her mistress's knee by one of the waiters—usually old Sayim the Nubian. All day long Milou cuddles Athène. Milou's manicured fingers have thickened, but she still wears her grandmother's heavy Russian rings. Her hands are mottled with liver spots, and they are uncertain on the cash register. They are heavy on Athène's back, stroking her smooth length, fondling the drooping ears, or scratching the worried brow as the old dog whimpers quietly.

Milou might have married Philippe, but that was long ago. Now, all day Milou watches the frayed red velvet curtains screening the entrance to the restaurant. She knows all her customers, though she never smiles and only nods sternly to the oldest and the most regular. The young tourists who stray in and park their backpacks by the door puzzle over this large, grim woman with the red hennaed hair who never leaves her seat. Yet despite the slight frown that Milou's features settle into when her thoughts wander, her customers find her a benign presence—and they come back.

To her left and slightly to her rear, so that she cannot see him unless she turns around, old Monsieur Vasilakis sits in a corner of the restaurant. He sits at a round table with a small black-and-white television flickering soundlessly on a cutlery cabinet in front of him and a carafe of red wine always at his elbow. Monsieur Vasilakis is nearing ninety, and almost all the friends who used to occupy the other chair at his table, share his wine, and stare companionably at his flickering TV have passed away. Milou usually knows exactly what he is doing even though her gaze is fixed in front of her. Today, it is Monsieur Vasilakis who is aware of his daughter's corner; the cash desk has been extended by a table with a white cloth, and a chair has been placed beside Milou's.

Milou observes the red curtains with particular purpose; she is expecting a friend. Well, Farah is too young to be quite a friend; her mother, Latifa, is really Milou's friend, and since their friendship dates from Latifa's wedding night, Milou has known Farah since she was born. Latifa's wedding night. Milou does not actually shudder or indeed feel anything much at all. But she remembers. She remembers the shame and the misery which for years that phrase had evoked in her; the shiver moving up her back into her shoulders and arms until her fingers tingled with it, the cold weight in her stomach that she had had to rub and press into something she could bear. Latifa's wedding night: when Milou had fled down the dark servants' staircase into Ismail Morsi's apartment to find his daughter, the bride, in the bathroom pulling off her veil and demolishing the elaborate chignon her hair had been pinned into. "I hate this," Latifa was muttering into the mirror, "and so does he. We'll wear the stupid clothes and sit on the platform to be stared at like monkeys, but I don't feel like *me* with this thing on my head and I am not having it." Then she had turned and seen Milou. She drew her in and bolted the door. She sat her down on the edge of the bathtub and made her drink some water and Milou told her everything. How strange that then it had seemed that she must die, that tomorrow could not happen. And now it was as though the whole thing were a film she had seen. A film that had moved her for a while.

Milou had first seen Philippe amid the ululations and the clash of cymbals at a friend's wedding in the Greek Orthodox cathedral on Shari el-Malika Street. Milou was twenty then. She was tall and well built and handsome. Her father, Khawaga

Vasilakis, sitting over his wine after their last customer had gone—watching her as she strode through the darkened restaurant folding up white tablecloths to take home for Faheema to wash—her father would often tell her then that she had her mother's shapely legs and her exuberant auburn hair. He always made this observation sadly. Then he would shake his head and bite the ends of his drooping gray mustache as he stared into his glass. Milou knew that her mother was French, had been a dancer, and had been beautiful—maybe still was. She had abandoned her husband and the one-year-old Milou for, of all things, a Turkish soldier: a black-eyed, whiskered brigand who had swaggered off his ship and into the Allied restaurant in Alexandria one fine day in '27 to wreck Theo Vasilakis's life. After three years of alternately swearing to smash the whore's face if she dared show it in the Allied and vowing that everything would be forgiven if only she would come back, for after all she was the mother of his child, Theo could bear Alexandria no longer. He sold the restaurant and took Milou and Faheema, the black maid who looked after them, to Cairo. He never saw his wife again and withstood all pressure to remarry. He opened Chez Milou (instantly "Shameelu" to the locals) on the rue Abd-el-Khaleq Sarwat and looked forward to the day when his daughter would be a partner and an adornment in the restaurant. Now that Milou was both, her father watched her constantly and lived in terror of the swashbuckler who would lure her away and ruin her father's patched-up life for the second and final time. For a swashbuckler it would have to be. You only had to look at the girl—the long, strong legs; the lean waist; the straight back; the broad forehead, wide-set eyes, and brilliant hair—to see the swarthy, muscled, sweating, tobacco-spitting son of a bitch who would claim her. Khawaga Vasilakis's paunch trembled with apprehension and distaste and he chewed on his mustache.

But Milou saw Philippe amid the incense and the burning candles in the Greek Orthodox cathedral and thought he looked like an angel: the boy—he could hardly be called a man—was so fair and so still. He sat at the far end of the pew on the other side of the aisle, the bridegroom's side. He was so separate that he appeared to belong more to the shining Byzantine icons on the walls than to the mass of breathing, moving people around him. Milou could see only his head in a three-quarter profile. His face was pale and fine-featured. Gleaming black hair rose smoothly from a white brow. His nose was chiseled; his mouth wide, his lips narrow and ascetic. She could not make out the color of his unmoving eyes. But it was a quality of serenity, a combination of his utter stillness and the way his head shone like an illumination in the dim cathedral, that so captured Milou.

Having no mother to do this work for her, Milou managed to find out who he was and—despite her dismay at confirming that he was indeed only seventeen and still at school with the Jesuits, the Frères—she contrived an introduction. Milou found that Philippe stood a few centimeters taller than her. She found that his eyes were green-gray and that his voice was mellow. His French was chic, more chic than her own, and his Arabic more broken. She found that even close up, his skin kept its luminous quality. She imagined that there was something extraordinary—extramortal, almost—about him, and longed to reach out and touch his face just on that fragile, contoured cheekbone and rest her fingertips in the shallow dips at the outer corners of his black-fringed eyes. She found out that he was the son of Yanni Panayotis, the grocer, and therefore that he was a neighbor of one of her father's oldest friends: Ismail Morsi, who owned a furniture shop in the market in Ataba Square.

Philippe bowed his head slightly, as though the better to hear anything she might say. He smiled, and his eyes said that something amazing had happened. Milou surprised herself; she had never before felt this rushing frailty, this tremulous energy, and it never occurred to her to wonder whether he had felt it too.

The year was 1946 and the victorious Allied soldiers were everywhere in the city. Khawaga Vasilakis thought his daughter showed remarkable acumen when she announced that since their business was doing well, it was foolish to go on buying provisions piecemeal from the neighboring shops. From now on, she declared, she would buy what they needed once a week, wholesale, from the market.

Yanni Panayotis's grocery was on the very outer fringe of the market—almost, in fact, in Shari el-Khaleeg, that wide road which until so recently would turn into a river in the season of the flood. Milou had never been that far from rue Sarwat before, and the first time she went, Faheema, who knew all the roads and the alleys of the city, went with her. They walked down King Fouad Street and stared in the windows of the *grands magasins,* then crossed Opera Square, through the very tip of the notorious Azbakiyyah District, across the busy swirl of Ataba Square and into the teeming, narrow Mouski. Faheema started to point out grocers' shops in the alleys along the way, but Milou would have none of them. It had to be Yanni Panayotis's store they went to, and his was the farthest one of all. Faheema, who was neither young nor green and whose breath was getting shorter as she hurried to keep up with her striding charge, began to grow suspicious. What would a grocery store have that would make a normally reasonable girl march ardently to the end of the world for it like this? There was only one answer possible. Faheema pursed her lips, collected her melaya around her, and puffed after Milou.

Yanni Panayotis was a big man with a great deal of shaggy black hair streaked with silver. He made up for his broadening forehead by growing a wild beard and mustache. He liked the looks of both women and sat them down in his dark, cool shop and offered them tea and chocolates. From then on, Milou always went to Shari el-Khaleeg on Sunday. She went one week and then the next, and the third time he was there. He was helping his father stack a delivery of large tins of white cheese. Milou sipped at her scalding tea and watched his broad back move under the fine white cotton shirt as he bent and straightened and lifted and reached. She glanced at the gray linen trousers shaping themselves around him as he squatted down in front of the cheese, but then she bit her lip and kept her eyes on the sawdust-strewn floor. When he had finished, Philippe took out a pressed white handkerchief from his pocket and wiped his brow. He was formal as he declined his father's offer of a cold drink. "I will leave you to conduct your business." He bowed over Milou's hand. "Enchanté, mam'selle, a most happy opportunity." He smiled into her eyes and left. Yanni turned to Milou, shrugging and spreading his hands wide, and saw at once her passion for his son in the girl's high color and rigid posture. Ah, so that's it, he thought. It is for this that it is Sunday, and always Sunday; the little Philippe has lit a fire.

"And what a fire that will be," he commented to his wife that night. "The girl is beautiful and her hair is in flames already." Nina turned down the corners of her mouth and pouted at the husband who—after two married daughters and a son who could, if he wished, grow whiskers and a beard—could still sweet-talk her back into bed with him on a Monday morning when the shop was closed and the boy had gone to school and Nina was in her flowered silk dressing gown, belted to show off her still-tiny waist. She would glance up at the mahogany display cabinet hanging in the corner above their bed with her bridal veil and its crown of orange blossom inside it and remonstrate that it was unseemly to behave like a honeymoon couple and draw the blinds in the morning after twenty-five years of marriage—what would the neighbors think? Khawaga Yanni grunted affectionately as he nuzzled his mustache into his wife's neck. "They will say, 'The old fool is still crazy for her,' and they will be right, no? Is that not so, little one? Ah, my little one . . ." and Nina would hold him gently and let him love her and think what a wonderful stew she would make for his lunch. Now she pouted and stared down at the petit point in her hand: the girl is too old; she is four years older than Philippe. Yanni should not be easygoing on such matters. A man can tire easily of a wife older than himself. Of course, on the other hand, she has no mother or brother to make trouble with, and when Monsieur Vasilakis— God grant him long life—goes, she will be the sole owner of a restaurant in a very good part of town.

The discussions continued and Milou's visits to the shop continued. Philippe left the Frères and joined the Faculty of Commerce and still every Sunday morning Milou would walk across town to the grocery store in Shari el-Khaleeg, take tea with Khawaga Panayotis, and hire a calèche to carry her and her provisions back to the rue Sarwat. Sometimes she began to despair, to lose heart, but then she would see him, and each time she was freshly convinced that he had "intentions"; their glance had met for a fraction longer, his smile had asked a question—a question she longed to answer. Until Latifa's wedding night.

Days before, Faheema, on the floor at Milou's feet with her mouth full of pins and her hands full of shiny emerald green taffeta, Faheema had urged her to make a move. "You either get him out of your head or you sort him out. A woman has to manage, you know. Three years have passed and it's 'I'm sure I felt him press my hand,' 'Today he actually touched it with his lips.' What is this dumb talk? Is this child's play or what? Maybe he's still young and doesn't understand how things work. Or maybe he has nothing for women. Some of your men are like that, you Greeks. Except—look at his father: there's a man for you, a man who fills his clothes. But you are not going to spend your whole life waiting. He doesn't speak? You've got a tongue. Make a little skirmish. See what clay he's formed of."

To get to the roof terrace where the wedding party was being held, guests had to go through Ismail Morsi's flat, out of its back door, and up the wrought-iron, unlit servants' staircase. The stairs had been freshly washed for the occasion and gleamed bright black in the darkness. The rubbish pails that normally stood on the landings had been kept indoors and the cats—who lived off the rubbish—stayed away. The large terrace was hung with lights and a marquee at one end provided a multicolored backdrop for the bridal dais. The drums beat out and the accordions wailed for all the neighborhood to hear and the hired, white-robed sofragis circled with silver trays of sherbet and chocolates and almond-filled sweets. Milou excused herself from the bride's younger sister Soraya and slipped away. Later, she tried to determine what had made her choose that particular moment, but she never could. She just remembered how she had leaned over and whispered a few words to Soraya; then, exchanging a look with Faheema, cross-legged with the other women servants on the carpet at the floor of the bridal bower, she had picked the skirt of her gown off the floor and headed for the stairs.

Milou turned a corner of the staircase and saw a man climbing out of the dark toward her. She stood still as Philippe, unaware, continued up the stairs. Then he must have heard a rustle or perhaps felt her breath, for he stopped. He looked up, and there it came again: the smile that barely touched his lips but shone through his eyes.

"Bonsoir!"

Never before and never again did Milou look as radiant as she did then: gathering her softly rustling dress, bare arms white against the green tulle of the bodice, her "Bonsoir" was the merest whisper. Philippe stood aside to let her pass, for of course he knew that it would be most improper to linger on the stairs. Milou lifted her skirt and stepped slowly down. The music pulsed down the stairwell. Milou drew level with Philippe. She turned as though to pass him sideways because of the narrowness of the stairs—and then she stopped. She was so close that she felt her breasts brush against him and her skirt fall around his legs. Milou lifted her face and his eyes looked into hers. She whispered his name and her hand let go of the crushed taffeta and rose to rest lightly against his cheek. Now, now he must surely . . . but Philippe, too well bred to step back, merely stood unmoving and Milou's hand drew away, went to her face, her throat, then clutched at the skirt again as she whirled around, ran down the stairs and into the bathroom, where Latifa was tugging the grips out of her hair.

Milou frowned at the red curtain opening to admit a very pretty young woman in a short-sleeved white cotton dress. She wore her sunglasses pushed to the top of her head and holding back her dark shoulder-length hair.

"Chérie!" cried Milou, and held up her hands. Athène woke up and growled deep in her throat.

"Tante Milou!" Farah said, bending to hug Milou's shoulders and kiss her on both cheeks. Farah sat on the chair next to Milou, asked a passing waiter for some iced water, fanned herself with a magazine, tickled Athène's ears, and began the ritual complaint about parking and the heat. "I've parked at the Opera and walked all the way up. But it is absolutely the only place and I'm going to see Tante Soraya later, so I guess it makes sense."

"She is still in your grandfather's old flat—God have mercy on him?"

"Oh, yes. She's still in Ataba. That's one thing that doesn't change, thank goodness. It's exactly the same as when my grandfather was alive. Even his bed is still there. Oh"—remembering—"shall I go and say hello to Monsieur Vasilakis? Or will I disturb him?"

"Don't bother," said Milou. "He won't know you anyway. He's become even more vague since Faheema died. He was used to her."

"God grant him long life."

"Ah, well, He is certainly granting him that." Milou nodded.

"But . . . things must be difficult for you, Tante Milou?" Farah said uncertainly.

Milou was silent, considering, her fingers on Athène's back. She was not smiling.

Farah stood up. "I'm going to go and greet him."

Milou did not look around as her guest bent over the old man and said his name gently. Watery, red-rimmed eyes shifted from the still-life of flowers on the television and looked up.

"I'm Farah, m'sieur. Do you remember me?"

Theo Vasilakis nodded several times and returned to the screen. Farah laid a tentative hand on his shoulder.

"They haven't changed this picture for three days," he complained. "Between every two programs this is what we get. They do have other tableaux: some with trees and some with birds—swans, you know." His hand moved in the air, wavering. "But they've been using *this* for three days. People can get bored. Eh. Well . . ." He watched the flowers re-signedly. Sayim the Nubian paused.

"It's all right, Sitt Farah," he said gently. "The khawaga is fine. You go and sit with Sitt Milou. See what you would like for lunch. The fatta is very good today—"

"I'm going to eat fatta, 'Am Sayim?"

"Yes, why not? Don't talk to me about a *régime*; you're as thin as a stick. You could do with some flesh on you. Go and sit and I'll get you a good lunch. Leave it to me."

Farah went back to her chair. Athène was asleep again, or at least her eyes were closed. Milou looked up and smiled. "So. Tell me, chérie, how is maman?"

"She's all right." Farah shrugged. "I guess she's happy where she is, away from us all."

"C'est dommage ça, her staying away like this. And it can't make things easier for you? Especially now?"

"No. Sometimes I'd like to talk to her. And it's harder living with my father when she's not there. Although I suppose in a way it isn't really, since they were getting on so badly. I don't know. Tante Soraya helps a lot, though, with the practical things—like looking after Adam for me. And I go and stay with her sometimes—for a break from being with my father. I feel much more comfortable at my grandfather's—at her place, really. You know, having grown up there and all that. But I can't really talk to her."

"She dotes on you. You've always been her child."

"But she's so bitter now. And sort of . . . hard. She's always irritated with Uncle—her husband. And she's completely disappointed in her son and tells him so all the time. She keeps pressuring me to go back to 'Adam's father,' and when I say we were unhappy together, she looks at me like I'm mad and says, 'So what? Who's happy in this world?' "

"Your mother seems happy—"

"Yes, but *she's* doing it all the wrong way around—discovering freedom and the pleasures of living alone now, after a million years of marriage. Still, she has a right. She says she reads in bed and she sleeps with the window open and she doesn't bother to cook but eats cheese and salads and fruit." Farah giggled.

"And Papa? He is not unhappy?"

"Oh, no. He's not bothered. I mean, I suppose he'd have preferred it if she'd stayed around and gone on being exactly as he wanted her to be. But since she started, you know, speaking up for herself, I guess he thinks he's better off on his own. You can't really tell with him, though."

"Aren't you going to have any lunch or what?"

Farah got to her feet. Monsieur Vasilakis was standing next to her.

"Well? Aren't you going to offer your friend something to eat?" The voice was querulous.

Farah glanced at Milou and answered quickly: "'Am Sayim is bringing me some lunch in a minute. Won't you join us, monsieur?"

"He's no use anymore, the old idiot. He's gone senile." Vasilakis was glancing around him as he muttered. Farah brought over a chair from the nearest table. "There you are, Monsieur Vasilakis. Please sit with us."

Now she was between the old man and his daughter.

"Where is the food for your guest?"

Farah glanced at Milou's set face and unease built up inside her, an old familiar unease. For years she had heard her grandfather use this tone to the daughter who had elected to stay and look after him. For years she had watched Tante Soraya's face set in just such a closed look as this one.

The waiter appeared with a tray. "That's the spirit, Khawaga!" He beamed. "You join the ladies and give the telly a rest. There's nothing on it but empty talk anyway, *and* it's all repeated." He set the dishes down in front of Farah. "I'll go get the khawaga's wine. Have a glass of wine, Sitt Milou, with the khawaga," he urged.

Milou shook her head. The carafe and a half-full glass were placed on the table. "Eat in good health and happiness." Sayim smiled at Farah. "You bring good company to us and light up our restaurant."

"And what about you?" Milou stroked Athène and continued as though there had been no interruption. "What about you, ma petite? Are you better off on your own too?"

"Oh, Tante Milou," sighed Farah, poking at the stuffed zucchini. "It's so difficult being a divorced woman here. I didn't think it would be this difficult."

"It's just because you haven't got your own flat," Milou lifted a hand from Athène and reached over to pat Farah. "When you have your own flat it will all be different."

"But I'm never going to have my own flat." Farah put down her fork.

"You've already bought a flat."

"Yes, but the man hasn't even started building it yet. It's all on paper. If he starts *tomorrow* it won't take him less than five years, and I'm practically thirty already. I really never thought it would be so difficult."

"Everything is difficult now. Everything," said Monsieur Vasilakis. He put down his glass and leaned forward, a hand on either knee. "Everything's changed. Life has become difficult. Very difficult." He shook his head. "In old times, it took fourteen different types of fish to make a bouillabaisse. I used to pick each fish personally. Nowadays what can you find? Three, four types maybe. Impossible to make a *vraie* bouillabaisse. Your father, he understood these things, he would tell me from the night before: Khawaga Theo, tomorrow we eat bouillabaisse."

"Papa, do you know who this is?"

"Eh? Of course I know who this is. Ismail Morsi's daughter."

"Ismail Morsi's daughter's daughter, Papa." Milou's voice was flat.

"I know, I know." The old man was impatient. "You've always been friends together, you two. Even though she married and you didn't." He turned to Farah. "Your daughter must be une belle demoiselle by now, eh?"

"Farah has a boy, Papa. His name is Adam. He's almost nine?" Turning to Farah.

"Almost. And he's utterly gorgeous. I would have brought him with me, but he's spending the day with his cousins. He's my whole life now, Tante Milou. I don't know what I'd have done if he wasn't with me. I can't imagine how some people go through life without ever . . . Oh, Tante Milou, I'm sorry—"

"It's all right, chérie." Milou patted Athène and scratched the dog's neck. "Don't worry. That's all in the past now. But what about il y a quelqu'un? Un homme?"

"Man, what man?" Monsieur Vasilakis had turned to see what was happening on television, but now he turned back, suspicious. "Aren't you married, child? My daughter herself went to your wedding."

Farah touched Milou's arm gently. "I am divorced, monsieur. My husband and I have left each other."

"Divorced, divorced, that is all one hears nowadays. Nobody has patience anymore." Monsieur Vasilakis sorrowed. "It wasn't so in our day. You waited. Maybe one partner makes a mistake. The other one waits. If one pulls a bit, the other lets go a bit. That way the world can go on. Life wants patience. Eh . . . so you're divorced? A waste of the money your father spent on your wedding. He had a big wedding for you, I know. Milou was there. A man who knew how to do things, your father: a proper man."

When her father had been silent for a few moments, sucking on the ends of his mustache and shaking his head sadly, Milou repeated quietly, "So, my dear. What about a man?"

Monsieur Vasilakis came to again. "Stay away from men." He looked earnestly at Farah. "Sons of bitches, all of them. They look impressive and inside they're worm-eaten. Leave them alone. Especially now. There *used* to be men. Why, the king himself used to dine here. And Eden. He ate at that table over there—with Montgomery. Anthony Eden, you know?" He nodded. Then he turned slowly in his chair to the television.

"I'm not interested, Tante Milou. No, truly. The few—two men, in fact—that I sort of *could* like are already married, firmly married. Other than that, I've had one proposal and you should have heard it: 'As for the fact of you being a divorcée, I am prepared to overlook it,' and he was supposed to be progressive. No. And besides, I don't want any conflicts around Adam. There was—" Farah paused. "I did think of an arrangement."

"An arrangement?"

"A marriage of convenience, I suppose it's called. I'm fed up with all the emotional stuff and I know I'm not going to be in love again; I don't want to be. But I do need a setup, I need somewhere to live."

"What are you talking about? This is a theory? Or there is a real person somewhere you are thinking of?"

"Oh, I'm not really thinking about it anymore. Yes, there is someone. But it's really too ridiculous."

"Is it someone from the club? An old friend from school? What is ridiculous?"

"Oh no, no, nothing like that. It's a neighbor . . . of Tante Soraya's. You might even know him."

Milou stared at Farah.

"Do you know him, Tante Milou? Monsieur Philippe? Panayotis? Tante Milou?"

"No. No, not really."

"Well, they've been Tante Soraya's neighbors forever. He's really quite old, I suppose. I don't know exactly *how* old. He doesn't look too bad, though, and he has a very gentle manner. Adam likes him. But I must say the main thing that made me think was the flat. They are magnificent, those flats, Tante Milou, aren't they? The high ceilings, the cornices, the long corridors. And *his* flat even has some amazing prewar wallpaper that looks as though it was put up yesterday. And then of course there's all that marvelous old furniture that his mother had when she was a bride absolutely light-years ago. Imagine. But I know it's wrong to think like that, and anyway there's something kind of spooky about it all. How come you've never met him, Tante Milou?"

"I have . . . met him. At occasions: weddings and so. That's all."

"Well, there is only him and Nina—that's his mother. He has sisters, but they've been settled in Greece forever and his father has been dead a long time. But Monsieur Philippe still lives with Nina. It's quite strange really, when you think of it, because Tante Soraya says that he's always had the same job since he graduated: some small accountancy job. She won't really talk about him, though—just says, 'Philippe never changes,' and that's the end of it. But she did tell me that he wouldn't take over his father's business when old Monsieur Yanni died."

"Yanni, eh? Old Yanni the grocer?" Monsieur Vasilakis only half turned around. "He was a good man too, God have mercy on him, like your father. We didn't see much of him here, but Milou used to buy all our groceries from him. Every week. He had a shop at the very end of the Mouski. Every week she would go there and come back with the groceries in a calèche. He gave her good discounts—for old customers, you know, Greeks together. His daughters went back to Athens, but he had a son too. A beautiful boy, they said, *and* he went to university. But we don't know anything about him."

"Didn't you like the fatta, then, Sitt Farah?" Sayim was disappointed at the pile of bread and rice left on the plate.

"It was delicious, 'Am Sayim, but I could never finish it. I'm afraid I picked out all the meat, though."

"This won't do, Sitt Farah. This won't do—"

"And I've eaten up all my vegetables." Farah smiled up at the old waiter, who was removing the plates.

Milou looked at Farah. "When you say you considered marrying . . . this man, he has asked you?"

"Oh, I'm not going to marry him, Tante Milou! I was just, you know, playing with the idea."

"But has he asked you?" Athène stood up and tried to get off her mistress's knee, but Milou held her by the collar.

"Oh, no."

"Well then?"

"But he would if I wanted him to."

"But he is Christian, Orthodox?"

"He would become Muslim."

"But how do you know? How do you know he would?"

"Tante Milou, one knows these things. There's definitely something in his eyes when he looks at me, and when I meet him on the stairs or he comes home from work and finds me chatting to Nina, he always looks as though something terrific has happened. I don't talk to Tante Soraya about this kind of thing, but Nadia, my youngest aunt, noticed and said she thought Monsieur Philippe had a tendresse for me."

"Nadia? Now she's really your father's darling, isn't she?" Monsieur Vasilakis was animated. "He would bring her in here when she was only so high and sit her properly at the table and let her order whatever she wanted! Ah! What a world! The last of the bunch is always pure sugar, as they say. How would I know? I only had Milou." Monsieur Vasilakis drooped again. He put out a shaky hand for his glass. "She was everything to me. Everything."

Milou held on to Athène's collar. "Tell me," she said, straightening up, "tell me. Suppose you thought a man had a tendresse for you, but he wasn't doing anything about it. And you wanted to hurry him up a little, so you made a move, an unmistakable move, one that nobody could pretend had been a misunderstanding. And he . . . he ignored it . . . ignored you. What would you feel?"

"It can't happen," answered Farah firmly.

"But if it did?"

"It can't happen. But if it did, then I suppose I shouldn't care for him after that. But it is a lovely word, isn't it, Tante Milou?"

"What? What is?"

"Tendresse."

"Ah," said Milou. "Tendresse . . . of course."

Melody

The scent of jasmine fills the air. It has been filling the air for the last month, I guess. Which is how you know the season is changing in this country. In this country the bougainvillea blooms against our walls all year round. The lizards dart out from under the stones and back in again. The mosquitoes buzz outside the netting and the pool boy can be seen tending the pool every morning from eight to ten. We're not allowed to use the pool—we women, I mean. It's only for the kids, and the men, of course. They can use anything. And they do. Use anything, I mean. And I don't get to smell the jasmine that much, either. You can only really smell it at night, and I don't go out that much at night because of Wayne. Not that there's anywhere to go, you understand. Only shopping or visiting in the compound. But even that I don't get much of. Wayne goes to sleep at eight. If he doesn't get his twelve hours he's a real grouch all the next day. And he has to wake up at half past seven in the morning to catch the school bus. Now, that's one thing I could never understand: why was the child never sent to school? She just kept her with her all the time. When we first came to this compound six months ago, they were the first people I saw. The first residents, that is. You don't count the maintenance people and the garden boys. We moved in on a Friday afternoon and the first thing we did was get right out again and drive up and down the road. I remember we said how convenient it was to have a grocery store, a newsstand, a flower shop, and a hospital right on our doorstep practically. Not that any of them looked like they were up to much, but still, they'd have to be better than nothing. And on Saturday morning, as Wayne and I came back from the grocery store (Rich—that's my husband—had gone to work, of course), we saw a woman and a child standing by the pool. The woman smiled and Wayne ran over. I followed. Mind you, I thought from the start she looked a bit tacky. Her hair was bronze, obviously dyed, and you could see the dark roots where it was growing out. She had quite a bit of eye makeup and her skirt was shorter than you normally see around here. She hadn't even bothered with an abaya, which is normally okay on a compound but not with such a short skirt. The kid was very pretty, though, and little Waynie fell for her straightaway. She was a true blonde with natural fabulous curls. Her face was heart-shaped with a pert little nose and big blue eyes, and she had drawn one of her mother's veils over her like a miniature abaya. It turned out she was only a couple of months older than Wayne. But she was much more self-conscious, self-possessed. Being a girl, I guess. Girls grow up quicker than boys. Well, Ingie, that was her name—the woman's, I mean—chatted away, although you couldn't really call it chatting since her English is appalling. She told me a bit about the compound and I asked where her kid went to school because I had to decide on a school for Waynie, and she said Melody did not go to school. She said she had another baby, Murat, who was asleep upstairs just then, and she was keeping them together and teaching Melody how to read and write. She said, "I like her with me." I thought right away that was wrong, although of course it wasn't for me to say, but the kid couldn't speak a word of English. She was very pretty and everything, and Wayne was standing there just staring at her all through our conversation. He was smitten. I think he just fell in love. Well, later that day when Wayne dropped his gun in the pool and I couldn't reach it and he's crying his head off, Ingie appears at her window and lowers a broomstick, yelling, "Try this, try this!" So we got the gun out of the water and went upstairs to give her back her broomstick and Wayne just would not leave; he had to stay and play with Melody. I never understood what the attraction was, quite frankly. She never played his kind of game. All she'd do was play with dolls and dress and undress them and talk to them—in Turkish. While he watched. And once I went to collect him and found them both sitting on the bathroom floor with bare feet and wet clothes, washing all the dolls' clothes. And Ingie just laughs and says, "It is so hot." Ingie's main thing is laughing. Laughing and clothes and makeup and dancing. And cooking. When we first moved in, she would come around maybe twice a week, each time with some "little thing" she had made: pastry, apple tart, pizza, whatever; things that take a lot of making. And little Melody was helping her. Melody also helped her, Ingie said, make all those tiny doll clothes for Barbie. I said, "But you can buy them at Toyland for practically nothing." She laughed and shrugged and said, "But I like." And I guess she likes cooking three-course meals and a sweet for her husband every night and waiting on him too, no doubt. The way these Muslim women treat their husbands just makes me ill. They actually *want* to be slaves. Mind you, of course, that's probably how she got him in the first place. I thought it was a bit odd when I saw him: a great big tall man, obviously a lot older than her. And, laughing, she tells me that they (Ingie, Melody, and Murat) are his second family. I pretend to be surprised, but in point of fact Elaine had already told me (Elaine is my Scots friend—she's been here for almost four years and she knows everything). Elaine told me he used to be married to an American woman and he'd lived in Denver for twenty years. They had two boys and he looked after them and did everything else as well. The wife worked and she had a strong personality and naturally she wouldn't do anything in the house. I have a lot of sympathy with that. I mean, housework and me are not best friends. I'd rather read a book. I do it here, though. Housework, I mean. Since I'm not working and

Rich is. But I don't like it. Anyway, Ingie's husband (he wasn't her husband yet at that point, of course), he had enough one day, so he packed up and went home and got himself a Turkish wife who would do absolutely everything for him. Then he brought her to this country where he could virtually lock her up while he made lots of money. We don't even know if he ever divorced his first wife. Ingie did not say any of this, of course. Just said he was a genius and loved his work and could fix any machine in the world and that his first wife is a "very bad girl" and that he is a "very happy, very joyful man." And indeed, their Betamaxes are there to prove it. Him dancing in front of family and friends at Melody's third birthday. A video of him filming Melody and a pregnant Ingie romping in the woods on a holiday in Vermont. All very joyful. Ingie too is a "very joyful person." When you visit her, she always has some tape on—loud. Disco, rock, oriental music, whatever. And one of Melody's favorite games is to sit Wayne down, get her mother to put on some of that wailing, banging stuff, grab a scarf, and start dancing for him. And she can dance. Arms and legs twirling. Neck side to side. Leaning backward. The lot. And Wayne, who normally can't sit still for a minute, sits trans-fixed, watching a little blonde who cannot speak a word that means anything to him, strutting and flirting about with a veil. I wasn't even sure this friendship was particularly good for him. But the tears and the tantrums that we had if I tried to stop him from going over—it was just easier to let him go. Once she was supposed to be coming to our apartment to play with him and she did not show. He just sat and waited. He wasn't even four yet, but he sat and waited for her for over two hours and then he made me take him to Ingie's apartment and when they weren't there, he sat down on the doorstep and wept. This whole compound, as far as he was concerned, was where Melody lives. Melody didn't care as much as he did, I think. But then she had a little brother and Waynie has no one. Well, he has three brothers, but they are much older and are back in Vancouver. In point of fact, we too are a second family. Rich was married for fifteen years. I don't really know that much about his first wife—except he pays her a lot of alimony, which is part of the reason why we're here. But he already had three sons and never wanted to have Wayne. Wayne was the result of a deal I made with Rich. When he got the offer of this job and he really wanted to take it, I said, "Okay, you give me what I want and you can have what you want." I mean, not every woman would agree to be buried alive in a place like this, would she? So he signed the contract and we bought the Jeep and set off overland, and while we were crossing France I got myself pregnant. He joked a bit about making sure it was a girl, but after Wayne came he really chickened out and went and got himself vasectomized so I could not nag him for another kid. Ingie said that her husband was waiting for their third. Always talking about it. But Elaine said Ingie had told her she was on the pill. She didn't want to get pregnant again because some fortune-teller back home told her she would have three children and one would break her heart. So she figured if she only had two, that would somehow invalidate the whole prophecy. I don't know about all that. I mean, I don't believe in fortune-tellers myself, but sometimes you hear stories of things they've said . . . Well, anyway, Ingie's husband was nagging her to have a third and every month he waited to see if she had conceived and meanwhile she's secretly on the pill and hiding the strip among Melody's pants and vests and terrified that he should find out. That's what these Muslim men are like; they can never have enough children. Mostly, though, they want boys. But this one wanted another girl. I asked Ingie how come he wanted a girl and she said he thought girls were more tender and loving than boys. Besides, a boy would always end up belonging to his wife, while a girl was "her father's daughter forever." "But," she added, "of course we believe everything God bring is good." Of course.

This was the kind of conversation you had with Ingie. She also knew everything about everything that happened, or—as was more often the case—that almost happened around the place: the children snatched, the near rapes, the Filipinos almost executed but deported instead, the German who went crazy. For all her tartiness, though, she was a good mom. They were both good parents, and you always found them in Kiddiworld on the last Thursday of the month—Western Family Day—and there would be this massive gray-haired Turk whizzing down the lighthouse slide with little Melody held tight on what Wayne called his "lamp" while Ingie waved at them, clutching Murat to her breast and laughing.

Now, of course, you don't see them there anymore. You don't see them anywhere, really. Even though they're still around. Well, nobody wants to see much of them to tell the truth. I mean, Elaine always said he was a bit weird, but I never knew *how* weird until I heard all that stuff about the camera. But of course I didn't know that until later. When it happened I hadn't seen Ingie for a while. I'd actually stopped going around that much. I still took Wayne there. But I'd leave him, then go and collect him. That night, though, I went. I had to. And the air in the compound was, as I said, not just full of the scent of jasmine, but literally heavy with it. It was eight o'clock and the older children were still out. Climbing the railings by the pool, running between the bushes, whispering, then a burst of laughter. I had to go. I knew that a lot of people had gone the night before and I'd watched people coming and going all morning and all afternoon. Well, that's maybe the Muslim way. But we usually just send a card. Or we go to the funeral. But I decided I'd better go or it would maybe look unfriendly. So I waited till I'd put Wayne to bed and I told Rich and I went out and it just hit me: how pleasant the night air was and how fragrant. I walked slowly because I had no idea what I should do or say once I got there. I looked up at their windows and they were all lit up and all the curtains wide open. I walked up the stairs and from outside the door I could hear the Qur'an being chanted, so I knocked and someone let me in and to the left were maybe twenty men sitting in a circle around a cassette player, silent. Screened from them, around the corner, huddled on the floor, a veiled woman, all in black, listened too. I stood unsure of what to do. Then the woman got to her feet and it was Ingie. She opened the door to the inner bit of the apartment, let me in, and closed the door behind us. She sat down on the sofa and I sat on a chair close to her. The apartment was full of women. Women and babies. Women sitting. Women making coffee. Women preparing food and handing it to the men outside. One woman was doing the dishes. Another was folding some laundry. All the women were in black. But the babies were bright spots of color. Murat—in red dungarees and a red and white shirt—hung on to his mother's knees for a moment and then propelled himself toward his sister's shiny blue tricycle. He fell, cried, was picked up and dandled by one of the women. I finally looked full at Ingie. I was all ready to find that she had aged overnight. But she hadn't. She seemed, if anything, younger. She had lost a lot of weight. I don't know how she managed it in only twenty-three hours, but she had, and she looked slight and frail in her long black skirt and her black T-shirt. No makeup, her hair pulled back and knotted with a rubber band, black circles around her eyes. Her skin—not just the skin of her face but of her arms, hands, and feet; all you could see of her—had grown finer, almost transparent. And she had lost her poise. Her movements were slow and awkward, adolescent. When she sat, her feet turned inward toward each other, like a shy girl or a twisted doll. Her eyes were red, and seeing me look, she pointed at them and whispered, "I have no tears." She also had no voice. Even her whisper had to be forced out. Every once in a while she would convulse in what looked like the prelude to a fit of weeping, but then nothing would come of it and she would just sit quiet again with a hand on either knee and her feet turned inward.

Staring at her fingers, she whispered, "People live fifty years. Seventy years, even. She lived fifty months." The woman sitting next to her on the sofa—a fat Egyptian who was perspiring so much you couldn't tell the sweat from the tears—pointed at the ceiling, then spread her hands, palms upward. Ingie whispered, "He gave her to me. Why He take her away? Why?" The woman reached over and patted the hand resting on the knee closer to her and said, "You are a Muslim." Ingie's voice rattled as she struggled to break out of her whisper. "I am Muslim. But she was my daughter." Then she went into one of her brief, dry-eyed convulsions. The woman patted her hand again and turned and spoke in Arabic to her own daughter hulking in black lace behind her. Ingie reached under a cushion and took out a pack of blue Silk Cut. Three Turkish women sprang up to get her an ashtray. After two drags and a whole lot of coughing she stubbed it out. Her white arms—no bracelet, no rings other than her gold wedding band—moved in dramatic gestures. "I cannot believe. From yesterday I am thinking, she will come from here, she will run from there. I see her run. I still hear her cry 'Mama!' A minute. All it is. One minute. I do it. *I* do it." She hit her breast. The Turkish woman Elaine says is her best friend stepped in from the kitchen and stood for a minute watching her. The Egyptian woman grabbed her hand and said, "But what happen? How it happen yesterday?"

"Yesterday," Ingie whispers like a machine, a robot with batteries running low, "yesterday we are at home all day. The children are restless. I take them to the shopping mall. My husband so tired, he not want to go. I say okay, we walk. We take my friend downstairs and her baby. We go. We make the tour. We give the children ice cream. We come back. Outside, I remember, no more Cérélac for Murat. I say to my friend: 'You keep the children. I run across the road for Cérélac.' " She looks around. "I don't want to take Melody in the shop. She always want chocolates and sweets and I think is bad for her. My friend say, 'Okay.' I cross. Then I hear Melody: 'Mama!' I turn and she is run after me and the car is coming so fast . . ." There is silence. She shakes her head. "I watching. He hit her, then the car carry her long down the road. Then she fall and start to go over and over. Everyone . . . they are running and the man from Jasmine flower shop, he carry her and we run to hospital, but she is die." Her hands fall on her knees and she looks around. Looks at me. Her eyes have a questioning, doubting look in them as though one of us might tell her she is wrong and Melody is not "die." The woman next to her murmurs in Arabic and two of the Turkish women—one with braids, round spectacles, and a fat baby and the other very classy, with perfectly painted nails and one of those serpent rings that cover a whole finger—have started to cry into some pink Kleenex. Ingie is rocking gently to and fro on the sofa while Murat leans against her legs and chews on a cucumber wedge. Melody's toys fill the room and a fat *Encyclopedia of Home Medicine* lies on the desk in the corner.

A little later, when I leave, I linger in the garden. I don't really want to go home just yet, and Rich is looking after Wayne for once, so I go to Elaine's. I can't stay with her very long because it's evening and Mike, her husband, is there, but I tell her about the scene at Ingie's and she says, "He never goes out weekends. He works all week and sleeps all weekend. Kids get restless." But as I say, I did see him in Kiddiworld.

When I left Elaine I decided to go across the road and buy some flowers, a surprise for Rich. I don't often do that kind of thing, but just to say thanks for looking after Wayne.

I cross the road. There are no marks on the surface, no bent lampposts, no police tape. Nothing to say that something out of the ordinary happened here last night.

The flower man, a greasy Lebanese I've never liked, said, "You have seen what happened last night?"

"The child?"

"Ah!" he said. "I saw it all. Nobody has a good view like me."

I chose five red roses and he started to strip them of leaves and thorns.

"I am standing at the door here. I see the lady cross. I know her. Often I see her. Always with the children. This time I see her cross the road and the other lady wait with the children. Then I see the little girl: she calls and runs. The mother turns and the car just *boom.*" He slams a fist into the open palm of his other hand. "Just *boom* and then carries her off: twenty-four meters. The mother is on the island in the middle of the road. Her arms are stretched out. But the screaming is from the brakes and the tires." He lays the roses carefully on a sheet of cellophane and bends to pick out some ferns to put with them.

"Me, I have started to run. The car drops her and she rolls over and over and she rolls into my arms like that. Blood is everywhere. I lift her. The head falls back and the eyes are all the way up so you can only see the white. But she is breathing. I hold her head against my chest and I run and run very fast to the hospital. The head, it is spurting blood at me—in pulses. Today, you know, I have asked my friend the doctor— he plays chess with me—I have asked him how much blood is a child, just four, having in her body? He says maybe four liters. Well, I tell you: it was four liters on me and I don't know how much on the road. I did not even notice, though, truly. I carried her to the hospital but she was dead. It was only later, when I have come back here, I start to smell. I look down and I am covered with blood." He wrapped some aluminum foil carefully around the stems of the flowers to keep them moist.

I said, "I heard her father rushed out and tried to kill the driver."

"Ah! But they stopped him. What good would it do? He was speeding, yes. But they all speed, and he was not expecting a child to run into the middle of the road at ten o'clock at night. He is in prison now and he will pay compensation, you know: blood money."

He tied a white ribbon around the cellophane-wrapped bouquet.

"He came here this morning with a video camera, the father. He was taking a film of the road. I went out to see and he made interview with me. He wants me to do exactly like what happened. Here the car hit her, like this. Here I pick her up, like this. I run like this. He took a whole film. Everything. The poor man."

I gave him his money and went home with the roses. I put them in a vase and told Rich all about it, but he was into some book and I don't think he really wanted to hear. Elaine did, though. I went to see her next morning as soon as I had put Waynie on the school bus. But all the while I was talking, I had a feeling she was keeping something up her sleeve, and sure enough, when I'd finished she said, "And you know what he did in the afternoon, the father? He went down to the morgue, where they were going to wash the poor child and lay her out, and he filmed the whole thing."

"But how could they let him?"

"They said the poor man was so crazed with grief it was better to let him do whatever he wanted. Besides, they're afraid of him; he's a big guy—and violent. And do you know what he did in the evening after you'd left and all the others had gone and only Ingie's best friend was there?"

Elaine leaned forward with her arms on her knees. "He sat Ingie down and made her watch both his videos: the one on the road and the one in the morgue. And then he made her watch the video of Melody's last birthday. He said what happened is her fault and she has to be made to feel it."

Well, that's weird. Weird enough for me, anyway. They also say he wants her to get pregnant immediately and give him another daughter. And she is not allowed to take little Murat out at all because he can't trust her to look after him.

Melody was in the morgue for a week while they got her an exit visa and he got leave from his work and then they all flew out to Turkey to bury her in their hometown. Elaine thinks that's morbid, but I kind of understand they wouldn't want to leave the kid here on her own when they finally go away. They had a bad time of it, though, because it was that freak five days when all of Turkey and Jordan were covered in snow and the drive from the airport to their hometown took ten hours. Still, I guess that was better than if it had been sweltering hot and all. Anyway, he blamed Ingie to everybody back home and she wanted to stay on with her mother a bit, but he brought her back because he wasn't going to leave little Murat in her care and because she had to get pregnant. And now they're here and it's all a bit spooky. No one quite knows how to talk to them, so we avoid them as much as we can. Everyone honestly thinks they ought to go away. But of course he's only done four years and he needs to do one more to qualify for the five-year bonus. We all understand that. But we don't understand her. How can she ever cross that road without thinking of Melody? How can she walk in the gardens? Live in the apartment?

That night I went to see her she suddenly leaned toward me and said, "She was . . ." Then she turned to the Turkish woman with the spectacles and asked something that appeared to be quite urgent. The Turkish woman looked serious and said, "Good. Not selfish."

"Yes," said Ingie to me very earnestly. "She was a good child. Not selfish. A good child."

"I am sorry," I said. "So sorry."

She stared at the carpet. "She was my daughter. Now my house is empty."

I patted her knee, the one the Egyptian woman wasn't patting. "You have Murat."

I left soon after that. Some women were leaving. Others were coming in. I didn't know it, but Ingie's husband was fixing up his videos. As I stepped out of the building, the air seemed fresher and the scent of the jasmine was even more strong. The children were still climbing the railings by the pool, buzzing with talk—and I remember wondering, how am I going to break the news to Waynie?

I Think of You

for Nihad Gad

I think of you often. I think of you often, and I remember. I remember, for instance, your old nanny coming into your room, the edges of her *tarha* caught between her teeth to hide half her face. Her eyes, filmed with cataracts, were so dim she must have been seeing you as though through a mist. I remember your husband turning from the phone, and the small gesture of your hand that stilled the impatient words on his lips. The old woman muttered indistinctly as she moved toward you, her arm describing cramped, arthritic circles with the smoking incense burner. Through the window, the darkness of the Cairo night was so intense, it seemed that if I reached out my hand I would touch black velvet.

Now the amber incense pervades this room, and as my eyes track the sweet cloud drifting behind the Baluchi cleaning woman, I see you once again sitting up in bed, splendid, your head wrapped in a turban of emerald silk. From the sofa I watched you: lit by a discreet lamp, your bed on a raised dais, a huge gray and white fur rug thrown over the bedclothes. In my light dress my body was warm with new life, but around your shoulders you drew a dark red woolen cloak and the fingers that held it to your breast were longer, more tapering than I had remembered, although still tipped in defiant scarlet.

Barbarian Queen, I thought then, Medieval Matriarch. Now, beached in this strange country, I wonder what these women among whom I find myself would make of you. Five women, each in a bed. They are dressed in grays and browns, garments fashioned so that underneath them they are all identical, solid bulk. Their hair is closely wrapped in dense black cloth, and more black cloth is folded back on top of their heads ready to veil their faces at a second's notice. My white cotton nightdress, smocked, buttoned to my throat, wide-sleeved with a frilled cuff touching the backs of my hands, feels light, revealing, beside the dark layers that they wear. My hair is uncovered and loose. I pull it back and twist it into a halfhearted braid and I feel the movement of my arms making my breasts shift under the cotton. I have nothing with which to secure my hair.

Your head was wrapped in emerald silk. The front still showed a narrow black hairline, but at the back, a thin, smoky tendril had escaped. Your son, fifteen years old, came in and wrinkled his nose at the smell of incense. Your old nanny slowly swung the burner into the corners of the room. Flat on the floor at the foot of your bed your dog lay; he flicked his tail and watched me with sad, uninterested eyes. Your son, before he left the room, climbed the dais to kiss you. Elevated, theatrical, your bed was worthy of Cleopatra; worthy of nights, afternoons, mornings of kingly caresses. And finally, of this.

I push my bare feet out from under the sheet and lower them from the bed. The perfect toenails I had once more achieved—twisting, bending, maneuvering around my now-enormous belly—are here ten small red badges of shame. And as my feet touch the floor, the nightdress slipping to reveal two ankles—swollen, but still ankles—the door of the ward swings open, a warning cough is heard, and a man walks in. Four hands fly up to four heads, four veils drop over four faces, and all sounds cease. Heavily I stand and reach for the curtains as the man, with lowered eyes, walks to the fifth bed and sits by his wife. I am not supposed to move, not supposed to move at all. But I walk slowly around my bed, drawing the green and yellow curtains, plucking at their edges, placing them carefully one over the other to complete my isolation. Awkwardly I climb again into the bed. I lie flat on my back and hold the sheet to my chin. I feel the tears well into my eyes and let them trickle coldly down my temples and into my hair. I do not want to be here.

Your hands were so thin and fine, a network of blue veins showed through the skin. Your eyebrows were carefully shaped: winged high above your deep black eyes. Your cheekbones (oh, how I always coveted your cheekbones) stood out now even more. Your mouth remained the same: wide and strong, the full lower lip tensing as you pulled your cloak more closely around you. Your mother, burdened by years and by her fear for you, stood for a moment in the doorway. Your husband lit another cigarette. You looked at the evening paper and talked animatedly about a review. I sat on the sofa and wondered how you could. But on the other hand, how else could you have been?

The Filipina nurse whisks the curtains apart and stands smiling between them. "You have to have some air. You will be too hot," she says, and briskly walks around the bed pulling them wide open. The man by the fifth bed has gone and the women are talking in low voices. The nurse picks up my wrist and stares at her watch. Then she puts my wrist down and shakes out a thermometer. As she puts the thermometer into my mouth: "You must not cry," she says on a melodious, rising note. Why you are crying? You will be all right."

Do you cry, my dear? I've never seen you cry. And yet I think I can hear the great, wrenching sobs—late, late in the night, when all the house is asleep.

One of the women gets out of her bed and walks around to the sink just outside my open curtains and hawks and spits, then runs the tap for a moment. She takes the two steps to my bedside and stands looking down at me. "Do not weep," she says.

I nod. So what if she spits into the sink? She didn't spit on me.

"Why do you weep?" she says.

I shrug feebly. If I open my mouth I shall howl.

"You do not speak Arabic?" she says.

"Yes, I speak," I say, but my voice comes out in a shaky whisper. I cannot make her out; with the shapeless smock and the wrapped head she could be anything from eighteen to forty-five. "Carrying, yes?" she says.

Again I nod.

"What is wrong with you?" she says.

I whisper, "High blood pressure."

"All things are in the hand of God," she says, and I nod. "Shall I raise your bed a bit?" she says. "You cannot be comfortable like this."

I shake my head; I do not want to be comfortable. But she cranks the bed up anyway so that my shoulders and head are raised up a little. She is being kind. Curious, naturally, but kind too. But I do not want to be comfortable. I do not want anything except not to be here.

I want to be with my daughter. Over the phone she asks, "Why do we have to be separated like this?" She is five years old and chooses her words with care and I want to be with her, treading water in the middle of a cool swimming pool, my circling arms breaking up the sun's reflection into patterns that form and re-form while she swims from me to the edge and from the edge to me again. I want to hold her foot as she sleeps—on her back, arms and legs flung out wide—and in the dim light, watch her eyes move under the delicate, slightly purple lids and wonder what it is she dreams of.

––––––

Standing at your window, I watched your driver and your old doorman kneel together inside your gate for evening prayers. I was sure they prayed also for you. In the street, a young couple loitered arm in arm in the crisp spring air and stared into a shop front glittering with fancy shoes. Beyond them, I could see the glow of Cinéma Roxy and I could almost feel the general hum as the open-air cafés of Heliopolis filled up for the evening. Your husband came up to the bed and looked at your drip. From the sitting room next door came the hum of conversation punctuated by the periodic click of the telephone followed by a chime as someone hung up and tried yet another number.

The Filipina nurse comes back with a young man in a white coat. The woman standing over me retreats to her bed. The doctor's stethoscope dangles close to my face. He says: "You must not cry, madam, it is not good for you." He speaks with a Syrian accent, his voice kind, and his eyes are a light hazel but too bright. I feel my mouth shape itself into a polite smile, and my hand lying by my side makes a slight gesture as though to say it's nothing.

"You must not be afraid," he says again. "All things are in the hand of God."

I nod and close my eyes briefly. I do not trust myself to speak. He stands and looks at me. His mouth smiles and his eyes burn. I wish I could make him less uncomfortable. I move my hand again.

My neighbor in the compound said, "You can have a crisis at any minute. If you're not in the hospital you'll die."

I said, "If I feel a crisis coming, I'll run to you for help."

"You won't be able to run."

"I'll walk then."

"It's not a joke," she said. "You have to go into the hospital."

"How can I go into the hospital?" I ask. "The exams are this week, I have to be with my students."

"You don't understand," she says. "I'm telling you: you'll die." In the end she brought me in for a checkup, and when they kept me, she took my daughter home with her. She looks after her and they phone me twice a day. When all is said and done, my daughter is the reason I would prefer to stay alive. She and this other, uncelebrated child inside me, clinging so tenaciously to life.

When your husband and the doctor left the room and we were alone, I climbed the two steps to your bed and picked up the hot-water bottle from where it lay on the fur rug beside you and said, "Wouldn't it be better under the cover?" I lifted the rug and the quilt and the blanket and the sheet and snuggled the bottle against you and covered you again. I put my hand on your shoulder and said, "Would you like me to rub your back?" And you sighed, "Oh my dear, I wish you would." I sat behind you. And when you allowed yourself to slump on to your side your spine touched my rounded belly and I felt the child inside me kick. I still don't know if you felt it too. I rubbed your back. Gently, gently with my right hand, my left elbow resting on your pillow, my left hand on your shoulder. It comforted me so, I could have rubbed for hours.

The doctor with the burning eyes hurries back carrying a hypodermic. He says, "Like this you are making your blood

I THINK OF YOU

pressure go up. I will give you some Valium. Could you please
roll up your sleeve?"

With my right hand I roll up my left sleeve.

The nurse says, "You want I do this?"

But he does not answer and eases the needle into my arm.
The Valium hurts as it enters the muscle. He pulls out the
needle and the nurse starts rubbing the tiny puncture with an
antiseptic wipe.

"You will sleep now," he says, and his mouth smiles.

My body is in pieces, each piece too heavy for me to support.
My hands are grotesque pads, the now-ringless fingers so stiff
I wonder at the time when moving them required no conscious thought. The wrists where I used to watch the shadowy
pulse throb under transparent skin are now dense, opaque
flesh. If I stretch out my arms and hang them through the rails
at the sides of the bed they are—for a while—not uncomfortable. The left arm hurts and I have to be careful with it or the
drip tubes will get tangled and blocked. My breasts are so
heavy they drag at the skin of my chest. I have to wear a bra
pulled high and tight. It cuts into my ribs and presses on my
lungs. Every few minutes I have to disengage my right hand
and lift the elastic and hold it away from me so that I can
breathe. When I hang my arm back on the railing, the relief of
not having to support it rushes through my shoulder and my
chest. What will they think when they come in and find me
like this: a suffering figure, arms stretched out to the sides? Or

do Christian images—even this one—not exist for them at all? They are probably not into images. Our religion is a religion of the Word, not of the Image. I close my eyes. Relax, they say. Relax, worrying is not good for you.

I am alone and this room is not unpleasant. There are no oranges or browns. The walls and bedclothes are white. There is a gray incoming-calls-only telephone by my bed and my mother, father, family call me from Cairo and my husband calls from London. There is a gray leather armchair. There is a television on a shelf in the corner; between it and the window there is a bilingual notice. The English reads: "Under no circumstance you must be alone with male doctor. Call sister urgently if male doctor approaches you for examination." I think this is funny and copy it laboriously into my notepad. I am alone and so, unobserved, I can hold on to what is left of me. Next to the notice I have pinned up the painting of a big, bright butterfly my daughter brought me on her first visit. I keep my students' exam papers next to me and correct them when I can.

In the morning the nurses detach me from the drip and I let myself carefully off the bed. I walk slowly across the room and into the bathroom. I pee with what precision I can into the waiting jug and cover it and replace it on the shelf. Although this is no longer the body I know, I wash it meticulously, spray it with eau de toilette, and dab moisturizing lotion on the bits I can reach. I brush my hair and do what I can with my face: I draw a black pencil along the puffy eyelids, apply some mascara and lip gloss. I put a bed jacket on over my nightdress. Back in the room, the bed has been made and the nurse helps me into it. She twitters that I should not get up, that I should use a bedpan, that I should let her wash me with a flannel. I smile politely and say nothing. She is very clean and neat with her white linen uniform and her small features and glossy black hair pulled back in a ponytail. She measures my blood pressure, my temperature, and my pulse rate, and notes it all down. She reattaches my drip and I lie back weak and nauseated but ready with my face, my bed jacket, my notepads and exam papers for the doctors' morning rounds.

They sweep into the room and position themselves at the foot of the bed. The consultant, majestic in his white robes and black and gold *abaya* stands center stage. The nurse hands him the notes and stands back. He looks at them and, slightly behind him, the Indian registrar with the slicked-back hair and a tightly shuttered face looks at them too. There is another doctor, Sudanese: Othello with a grieving face and a limp and an ebony cane. Three local house doctors stand farther back. They are women and all I can see of them is their dark eyes through the slits of their black veils.

When they go, the nurse asks if my arm is stiff. She whispers that it was wrong of the doctor to put the Valium in my arm. "It should be here," she says, patting my hip, "but he was afraid to ask you. The muscle in the arm is not so big."

Your back was so thin; through the flannel nightgown and the woolen cloak I could feel each vertebra. I rubbed slowly down your spine and out and up in a circle and pressed your shoulder and your neck, then went down your spine again. I could have cradled you like a baby. I could have kissed your head and your hands and wept over you. But I sat behind you and rubbed your back and thought, Tomorrow I leave. Will you still be here when I come back in the summer? I wanted to tell you things and ask you things. I said, "Do you remember when we had lunch at the Meridien seven years ago?"

"You should not go downstairs," the nurse says at five o'clock as she disengages my drip.

"You don't allow children up here," I reply. I ease myself off the bed and wrap my body in the black *abaya* and my head in the black *tarha* and walk slowly out of the door.

In the women's corner of the vast waiting area on the ground floor my daughter climbs on to my knee. She strokes my uncovered face and I bury my mouth in her small, plump palm. She plants big wet kisses on my eyes, my cheeks, my nose, and my mouth. A group of women sitting silently nearby stare at us through their veils.

On my fourth day, the door of my room opens and a woman walks in. She is tall and wears a long, loose gray garment with buttons up the front and the usual black veil over her face and head. In her hand she carries a covered dish. She looks around to make sure I am alone in the room. "There are no men?"

"There are none."

She lifts the veil from her face and lays it back on top of her head. "Peace be upon you!"

"And upon you peace and the mercy of God and His blessings."

She puts the dish on the cabinet next to the phone and settles into the gray armchair. She has a young but not particularly fine face. She wears, of course, no makeup.

"I have brought you something to support you, sister. Hospital food is tasteless."

"May God increase your bounty," I say. "It was not necessary to trouble yourself."

"We see no one comes to visit you?"

"I have no people here."

As I say the words, I feel tears of self-pity well up behind my eyes. But I blink them away. I can do this much.

"They say you are married to an Englishman?"

"It is true."

"But how can you marry an Englishman?"

"It is my portion and my fate."

"But you are Muslim. How can you marry an Englishman?"

"He has embraced our religion."

"And you live there?"

"Yes."

"How can you live there? They are all animals there."

"They are people, like us."

"They live like animals there."

"They live like us. Among them there is good and there is bad."

"They copulate on the streets there."

"Pardon?"

"There, the people copulate on the streets."

"I have lived there a long time; I never saw anybody copulating on the street."

"I saw it."

"Where?"

"In films. My husband brings home video films and I have seen them: the man goes to the woman on the street, he lifts her clothes and copulates with her."

"Ah! Those films don't represent the truth. They are made only to excite people's appetites."

"I have to go," she says, and rises. "But your husband is a good man? He is good to you?"

"Like my own people."

"My husband is a teacher."

"It is a good profession."

"Peace be upon you!" She pulls the veil down over her face and moves toward the door.

"And upon you peace," I say, "and thank you for your generous gift."

We had taken refuge from the July heat in the air-conditioned coffee shop of the Cairo Meridien. We drank chilled white wine and ate tomato and white cheese salad and artichokes vinaigrette. Your first play was a rave and people turned to look at you as they walked past. We watched the sun sparkle silver on the Nile at its widest point and we peeled the leaves off the artichokes and ate their pale green hearts and I told you of all the ways I loved him and you listened. Then I told you of how, when I had the flu, he had tended me like a mother.

"He even read me a silly little fairy story," I said, "to cheer me up."

You said, "Marry him."

I said, "But how will I manage never to speak to him in my own language? How can I stand not to live here?"

"Cairo will always be there for you," you said.

On the sixth day the Scottish matron comes in and rechecks my pulse. She says I should have morphine and should not go downstairs anymore. I say, "But you don't allow children up here, and I have to see my daughter."

She says my body is like a compression chamber and every move I make adds to the pressure on my baby.

"What about tension?" I say. "What about misery? What about loneliness?"

"They are animals, these people," she says, "animals. They don't understand a thing. They think if they have rules, it makes them civilized. But never mind, pet. You just think of your baby and be a good girl and we'll have you out of here very soon."

My students phone me and send me flowers and fruit. They offer to take my little girl to their houses to swim, to play with their children. But no one can bring her here to me.

My husband phones me every day. He has tried to get a visa to come over, but they tell him it has to be sent from this end and will take at least three weeks. "You'll be out of that damned place then, won't you?" he says. "You'll be home."

I correct my exam papers, and after each question I have to stop to take my breath and pluck at the elastic of my bra.

―――――

Outside, after I left you, I looked up at your house—your father's house and his father's before him—and it was ablaze with lights. And there in the street, I hugged my old friend, your husband, and the doorman turned away and wiped his face with his wide sleeve.

My mother phones and tells me you have been to America and back, and no, you are not better. Do you think of death? You must do. You must know you are dying. Half your stomach taken out, the needle plastered to your hand ready for your next feed. Your brother scouring the medical depots for supplies, your doctors on twenty-four-hour rotations, your family coming and going and no one ever mentioning the dread name of your disease. All the talk was of ulcers and vague complications and exploratory surgery, not of the removal of chunks of stomach and yards of intestine—not of the disease that maneuvers like mercury, finding fresh footholds as the old are cut away. You must know. Your husband said you did not. He said it was better like this, you would not be able to take it. Is this the last kindness you are doing him, allowing him to believe you do not know? Playing it his way to the end? Letting him off grand finales and anguished summings-up?

For three days my mother does not call. When on my tenth day in this room she calls and I ask after you, she begs me not to take it too badly, to think of my blood pressure, to think of my baby, to think of my daughter. Every possible thing was done. There was nothing more anybody could do.

A nurse comes in with the Sudanese doctor. She stands by as he bends over me. He slips his hand under the cover and speaks kindly. "What are you doing to your blood pressure? I will try not to hurt you. Yes, you are dilating. We want to try to hurry things up. Your blood pressure is much too high. It is all this crying. Why do you make yourself so unhappy? But it may still be possible to have a normal delivery."

"Is the baby all right?" I ask.

"You are in the eighth month. God willing, the baby will be fine."

He rims between my legs three times with hard fingers and a nurse hurries in to listen with her black box at the wall of my belly.

On the back of your hand I saw the needle go into the blue vein. In my hand all detail has vanished; the tube disappears under a spaghetti junction of bloodied plaster. I lie and listen out for the movements of my baby, for the little left hooks to my liver or the flurry of kicks that precedes him falling asleep in a tight ball that wrenches my whole body to one side. He does not move and I imagine him gasping for breath as the cord that connects us fails to deliver the oxygen he needs. No, as *I* fail to deliver the oxygen he needs. I carefully disengage my arm from the railing and rub slowly along the side of my belly, coaxing him, willing him to wake, to kick. I try not to think of you, and as I cast about for other thoughts, I feel the tears on my face while image after unbearable image presents itself to my mind. Five years ago, sitting in the Paprika with my husband when he was still in love with me, he caught my hand across the table and raised it to his mouth. In the car, in the desert, he pushed his hand between my thighs. I want, I want to be five years old and playing in the sunshine on my grandmother's carpet. I want to be at my nineteenth birthday party with all my friends and you, newly wed, dancing into the room with an armful of white lilies and blue irises. I want to be home. When I turn my head I see, out of the window, a woman cross the parking lot in the glaring sun. Her black *abaya* billows out around her and she clutches at it and bends forward as she fights the dust-laden wind.

In the dead of night my phone rings. As I reach for it in the dark I try to still my heart, for I imagine each startled beat adding to the pressure on my baby. What more can happen now? A man's voice, speaking low, calls me by name. An admirer, he says, a well-wisher, one of your doctors, he says. If he spoke in Arabic I could tell which one by his accent, but he speaks only English to me. He says, "I know you cannot leave your bed. Would you like me to be with you? Your breasts are very big now. They hurt you, don't they? If I suck them I can make them better." I put the phone down and he rings again and again. I keep the phone off the hook, but if my daughter needs me, if something should happen—I put the receiver back.

When it came, it came suddenly, just as my neighbor—my savior, it turns out—had said it would. How could I, who had been stalked for so long, still be taken so completely by surprise?

On the eleventh day my daughter on the phone asked, "Do you still like the butterfly I gave you?"

"Yes, darling," I said.

"Will it always be nice for you?" she asked.

"Of course it will," I said.

"And you won't ever hate it *ever*, will you?"

"Of course not, sweetheart," I said. "I adore it."

I turned my head to negotiate the tubes and replace the receiver and felt a muffled rush as though I sensed a distant sea breaking against rock. As the receiver dropped, I was pushed under by the rushing waves.

Of the time after, fragments only remain. My teeth chattering so hard that my skull reverberated with the sound. Cloth wedged into my mouth, then removed as I started to retch. My stomach empty, but a thin stream of bile continuing to eject itself in bitter spurts through my throat. The wetness flowing from me, whether it was water or blood I never knew. The rhythmic blows behind my eyes that shook my body. And voices talking to me, and hands, hands holding, mopping, wiping, carrying me. And then a room with a fierce white light and Othello and the mad-eyed Syrian and other figures busy around me and a churning and grinding kneading my body from waist to groin and needles going into my arms and back and a voice in my ear saying, "Your husband is on the phone. He wants you to know that he is with you always," and a matador in overalls and a mask and shower cap braced between my legs and the white light burning, burning into all the pain and noise until an angel in a black veil dimmed it and turned it away from my face and came and bent over me and I must have said something, for she said, "Have courage, sister. I shall not leave you," and she held my hand and the ankle of one splayed leg and every time I slipped under that roaring tide I floated up again to hear her soft recitative, her unending verses of Qur'anic comfort.

He fought his way out, my brave baby boy, and they took him away to an incubator, warm and silent and still as I could not be. And they worked hard at me for what I later learned were three nights and three days until at last, as I lay once again in my old bed, empty and clean and calm, they delivered to me a warm, soft bundle. And holding it close, I folded back the flowered wrappings and saw for myself the breathing brown body, the cut cord, the downy head, the long, black lashes, the curled fingers, and my name on the tag around his wrist.

My daughter on the phone says, "Tomorrow we're coming to get you."

I say, "I know. I can't wait."

"Have you finished your exams?" she asks.

"Yes," I say, "they're done."

"Then we can go home," she says, "because we have to show the baby to Daddy."

"Absolutely," I say. "Absolutely, sweetheart."

In the Meridien, all those years ago, with the Nile shining behind you, I said, "But you've been married nine years. Can one trust passion, romance? Can one really trust being in love?" A shadow passed across your face. "Well," you said after a moment, "of course things change. Yes, they do. But I think now, perhaps, sympathy—yes, sympathy and tenderness and goodwill. *They* can last, if we're wise. Maybe they are the lasting part of love. My husband has those. And your man, from what you say, has them too."

You had everything I wanted: confidence, high cheekbones, a long-running play, a happy—well, comparatively happy—second marriage. I think of you on Friday nights, the door of your lit-up house open onto the garden, the garden gate open onto the road. You move between your guests, your husband, your pets, your children, your mother, your servants. You make conversation, drinks, and food, and I watch you lightly draw the fine-lined patterns that pull so many lives together. My dear, oh, my dear, you made it look so easy.

Sandpiper

Outside, there is a path. A path of beaten white stone bordered by a white wall—low, but not low enough for me to see over it from here. White sands drift across the path. From my window, I used to see patterns in their drift. On my way to the beach, I would try to place my foot, just the ball of my foot, for there never was much room, on those white spaces that glinted flat and free of sand. I had an idea that the patterns on the stone should be made by nature alone; I did not want one grain of sand, blown by a breeze I could not feel, to change its course because of me. What point would there be in trying to decipher a pattern that I had caused? It was not easy. Balancing, the toes of one bare foot on the hot stone, looking for the next clear space to set the other foot down. It took a long time to reach the end of the path. And then the stretch of beach. And then the sea.

I used to sit where the water rolled in, rolled in, its frilled white edge nibbling at the sand, withdrawing to leave great damp half-moons of a darker, more brownish beige. I would sit inside one of these curves, at the very midpoint, fitting my body to its contour, and wait. The sea unceasingly shifts and stirs and sends out fingers, paws, tongues to probe the shore. Each wave coming in is different. It separates itself from the vast, moving blue, rises and surges forward with a low growl, lightening as it approaches to a pale green, then turns over to display the white frill that slides like a thousand snakes down upon itself, breaks and skitters up the sandbank. I used to sit very still. Sometimes the wave would barely touch my feet, sometimes it would swirl around me, then pull back, sifting yet another layer of sand from under me, leaving me wet to the waist. My heels rested in twin hollows that filled, emptied, and refilled without a break. And subtle as the shadow of a passing cloud, my half-moon would slip down the bank—only to be overtaken and swamped by the next leap of foaming white.

I used to sit in the curve and dig my fingers into the grainy, compact sand and feel it grow wetter as my fingers went deeper and deeper till the next rippling, frothing rush of white came and smudged the edges of the little burrow I had made. Its walls collapsed and I removed my hand, covered in wet clay, soon to revert to dry grains that I would easily brush away.

I lean against the wall of my room and count: twelve years ago, I met him. Eight years ago, I married him. Six years ago, I gave birth to his child.

For eight summers we have been coming here; to the beach house west of Alexandria. The first summer had not been a time of reflection; my occupation then had been to love my husband in this—to me—new and different place. To love him as he walked toward my parasol, shaking the water from his black hair, his feet sinking into the warm, hospitable sand. To love him as he carried his nephew on his shoulders into the sea, threw him in, caught him and hoisted him up again—a colossus bestriding the waves. To love him as he played backgammon with his father in the evening, the slam of counters and clatter of dice resounding on the patio while, at the dining room table, his sister showed me how to draw their ornate, circular script. To love this new him, who had been hinted at but never revealed when we lived in my northern land, and who after a long absence had found his way back into the heart of his country, taking me along with him. We walked in the sunset along the water's edge, kicking at the spray, my sun hat fallen on my back, my hand, pale bronze in his burnt brown, my face no doubt mirroring his, aglow with health and love—a young couple in a glitzy commercial for a two-week break in the sun.

My second summer here was the sixth summer of our love—and the last of our happiness. Carrying my child and loving her father, I sat on the beach, dug holes in the sand, and let my thoughts wander. I thought about our life in my country before we were married: four years in the cozy flat, precarious on top of a roof in a Georgian square: his meeting me at the bus stop when I came back from work; Sundays when it did not rain and we sat in the park with our newspapers; late nights at the movies. I thought of those things and missed them, but with no great sense of loss. It was as though they were all there to be called upon, to be lived again whenever we wanted.

I looked out to sea and, now I realize, I was trying to work out my coordinates. I thought a lot about the water and the sand as I sat there watching them meet and flirt and touch. I tried to understand that I was on the edge, the very edge of Africa; that the vastness ahead was nothing compared to what lay behind me. But even though I'd been there and seen for myself its never-ending dusty green interior, its mountains, the big sky, my mind could not grasp a world that was not present to my senses. I could see the beach, the waves, the blue beyond, and cradling them all, my baby.

I sat with my hand on my belly and waited for the tiny eruptions, the small flutterings that told me how she lay and what she was feeling. Gradually we came to talk to each other. She would curl into a tight ball in one corner of my body until, lopsided and uncomfortable, I coaxed and prodded her back into a more centered, relaxed position. I slowly rubbed one corner of my belly until *there,* aimed straight at my hand, I felt a gentle punch. I tapped and she punched again. I was twenty-nine. For seventeen years my body had waited to conceive, and now my heart and mind had caught up with it. Nature had worked admirably; I had wanted the child through my love for her father, and how I loved her father that summer. My body could not get enough of him. His baby was snug inside me and I wanted him there too.

From where I stand now, all I can see is dry, solid white. The white glare, the white wall, and the white path, narrowing in the distance.

I should have gone. No longer a serrating thought but familiar and dull. I should have gone. In that swirl of amazed and wounded anger when, knowing him as I did, I first sensed that he was pulling away from me, I should have gone. I should have turned, picked up my child, and gone.

I turn. The slatted blinds are closed against a glaring sun. They call the wooden blinds *sheesh* and tell me it's the Persian word for glass. So that which sits next to a thing is called by its name. I have had this thought many times and feel as though it should lead me somewhere, as though I should draw some conclusion from it, but so far I haven't.

I draw my finger along a wooden slat. Um Sabir, my husband's old nanny, does everything around the house, both here and in the city. I tried at first at least to help, but she would rush up and ease the duster or the vacuum cleaner from my hands. "Shame, shame. What am I here for? Keep your hands nice and soft. Go and rest. Or why don't you go to the club. What have you to do with these things?" My husband translated all this for me and said things to her which I came to understand meant that tomorrow I would get used to their ways. The meals I planned never worked out. Um Sabir cooked what was best in the market on that day. If I tried to do the shopping the prices trebled. I arranged the flowers, smoothed out the pleats in the curtains, and presided over our dinner parties.

My bed is made. My big bed into which a half-asleep Lucy, creeping under the mosquito net, tumbles in the middle of every night. She fits herself into my body and I put my arm over her until she shakes it off. In her sleep she makes use of me; my breast is sometimes her pillow, my hip her footstool. I lie content, glad to be used. I hold her foot in my hand and dread the time—so soon to come—when it will no longer be seemly to kiss the dimpled ankle.

On a black leather sofa in a transit lounge in an airport once, many years ago, I watched a Pakistani woman sleep. Her dress and trousers were a deep yellow silk, and on the dress bloomed luscious flowers in purple and green. Her arms were covered in gold bangles. She had gold in her ears and in her left nostril, gold around her neck. Against her body her small son lay curled. One of his feet was between her knees, her nose was in his hair. All her worldly treasure was on that sofa with her, and so she slept soundly on. That image too I saved up for him.

I made my bed this morning. I spread my arms out wide and gathered in the soft, billowing mosquito net. I twisted it around in a thick coil and tied it into a loose loop that dangles gracefully in midair.

Nine years ago, sitting under my first mosquito net, I had written: "Now I know how it feels to be a memsahib." That was in Kano, deep, deep in the heart of the continent I now sit on the edge of. I had been in love with him for three years, and being apart then was merely a variant of being together. When we were separated, there was for each a gnawing lack of the other. We would say that this confirmed our true, essential union. We had parted at Heathrow, and we were to be rejoined in a fortnight in Cairo, where I would meet his family for the first time.

I had thought to write a story about those two weeks; about my first trip into Africa: about Muhammad al-Senusi explaining courteously to me the inferior status of women, courteously because, being foreign, European, on a business trip, I was an honorary man. A story about traveling the long, straight road to Maiduguri and stopping at roadside shacks to chew on meat that I then swallowed in lumps while Senusi told me how the meat in Europe had no body and melted like rice pudding in his mouth. About the time I saw the lion in the tall grass. I asked the driver to stop, jumped out of the car, aimed my camera, and shot as the lion crouched. Back in the car, unfreezing himself from horror, the driver assured me that the lion had crouched in order to spring at me. I still have the photo: a close-up of a lion crouching in tall grass. I look at it and cannot make myself believe what could have happened.

I never wrote the story, although I still have the notes. Right here in this leather portfolio which I take out of a drawer in my cupboard. My Africa story. I told it to him instead— and across the candlelit table of a Cairo restaurant he kissed my hands and said, "I'm crazy about you." Under the high windows the Nile flowed by. Eternity was in our lips, our eyes, our brows. I married him, and I was happy.

I leaf through my notes. Each one carries a comment, a description meant for him. All my thoughts were addressed to him. For his part, he wrote that after I left him at the airport he turned around to hold me and tell me how desolate he felt. He could not believe I was not there to comfort him. He wrote about the sound of my voice on the telephone and the crease at the top of my arm that he said he loved to kiss.

What story can I write? I sit with my notes at my writing table and wait for Lucy. I should have been sleeping. That is what they think I am doing. That is what we pretend I do: sleep away the hottest of the midday hours. Out there on the beach, by the pool, Lucy has no need of me. She has her father, her uncle, her two aunts, her five cousins; a wealth of playmates and protectors. And Um Sabir, sitting patient and watchful in her black galabiya and *tarha,* the deck chairs beside her loaded with towels, sun cream, sun hats, sandwiches, and iced drinks in thermos flasks.

I look and watch and wait for Lucy.

In the market in Kaduna the mottled red carcasses lay on wooden stalls shaded by gray plastic canopies. At first I saw the meat and the flies swarming and settling. Then on top of the gray plastic sheets, I saw the vultures. They perched as sparrows would in an English market square, but they were heavy and still and silent. They sat cool and unblinking as the fierce sun beat down on their bald, wrinkled heads. And hand in hand with the fear that swept over me was a realization that fear was misplaced, that everybody else knew they were there and still went about their business; that in the meat market in Kaduna, vultures were commonplace.

The heat of the sun saturates the house; it seeps in through every pore. I open the door of my room and walk out into the silent hall. In the bathroom I stand in the shower and turn the tap to let the cool water splash over my feet. I tuck my skirt between my thighs and bend to put my hands and wrists under the water. I press wet palms to my face and picture gray slate roofs wet with rain. I picture trees—trees that rustle in the wind, and when the rain has stopped, release fresh showers of droplets from their leaves.

I pad out on wet feet that dry by the time I arrive at the kitchen at the end of the long corridor. I open the fridge and see the chunks of lamb marinating in a large metal tray for tonight's barbecue. The mountain of yellow grapes draining in a colander. I pick out a cluster and put it on a white saucer. Um Sabir washes all the fruit and vegetables in red permanganate. This is for my benefit, since Lucy crunches cucumbers and carrots straight out of the greengrocer's baskets. But then she was born here. And now she belongs. If I had taken her away then, when she was eight months old, she would have belonged with me. I pour out a tall glass of cold bottled water and close the fridge.

I walk back through the corridor. Past Um Sabir's room, his room, Lucy's room. Back in my room I stand again at the window, looking out through the chink in the shutters at the white that seems now to be losing the intensity of its glare. If I were to move to the window in the opposite wall I would see the green lawn encircled by the three wings of the house, the sprinkler at its center ceaselessly twisting, twisting. I stand and press my forehead against the warm glass. I breathe on the windowpane, but it does not mist over.

I turn on the fan. It blows my hair across my face and my notes across the bed. I kneel on the bed and gather them. The top one reads: "Ningi, his big teeth stained with kola, sits grandly at his desk. By his right hand there is a bicycle bell he rings to summon a gofer," and then again: "The three things we stop for on the road should be my title: 'Peeing, Praying, and Petrol.' " Those were lighthearted times, when the jokes I made were not bitter.

I lie down on the bed. These four pillows are my innovation. Here they use one long pillow with two smaller ones on top of it. The bed linen comes in sets. Consequently my bed always has two pillows in plain cases and two with embroidery to match the sheets. Also, I have one side of a chiffonier full of long, embroidered pillowcases. When I take them out and look at them I find their flowers, sheltered for so long in the dark, are unfaded, bright, and new.

Lying on the bed, I hold the cluster of grapes above my face and bite one off as Romans do in films. Oh, to play, to play again, but my only playmate now is Lucy, and she is out by the pool with her cousins.

A few weeks ago, back in Cairo, Lucy looked up at the sky and said, "I can see the place where we're going to be."

"Where?" I asked as we drove through Gabalaya Street.

"In heaven."

"Oh!" I said. "And what's it like?"

"It's a circle, Mama, and it has a chimney, and it will always be winter there."

I reached over and patted her knee. "Thank you, darling," I said.

Yes, I am sick, but not just for home. I am sick for a time, a time that was and that I can never have again. A lover I had and can never have again.

I watched him vanish—well, not vanish, slip away, recede. He did not want to go. He did not go quietly. He asked me to hold him, but he couldn't tell me how. A fairy godmother, robbed for an instant of our belief in her magic, turns into a sad old woman, her wand into a useless stick. I suppose I should have seen it coming. My foreignness, which had been so charming, began to irritate him. My inability to remember names, to follow the minutiae of politics; my struggles with his language; my need to be protected from the sun, the mosquitoes, the salads, the drinking water. He was back home, and he needed someone he could be at home with, at home. It took perhaps a year. His heart was broken in two; mine was simply broken.

I never see my lover now. Sometimes as he romps with Lucy on the beach or bends over her grazed elbow or sits across our long table from me at a dinner party, I see a man I could yet fall in love with, and I turn away.

I told him too about my first mirage, the one I saw on that long road to Maiduguri. And on the desert road to Alexandria the first summer, I saw it again. "It's hard to believe it isn't there when I can see it so clearly," I complained.

"You only think you see it," he said.

"Isn't that the same thing?" I asked. "My brain tells me there's water there. Isn't that enough?"

"Yes," he said, and shrugged. "If all you want to do is sit in the car and see it. But if you want to go and put your hands in it and drink, then it isn't enough, surely?" He gave me a side-long glance and smiled.

Soon I should hear Lucy's high, clear voice, chattering to her father as they walk hand in hand up the gravel drive to the back door. Behind them will come the heavy tread of Um Sabir. I will go out smiling to meet them and he will de-liver a wet, sandy Lucy into my care and ask if I'm okay with a slightly anxious look. I will take Lucy into my bathroom while he goes into his. Later, when the rest of the family have all drifted back and showered and changed, everyone will sit around the barbecue and eat and drink and talk politics and crack jokes of hopeless, helpless irony and laugh. I should take up embroidery and start on those Aubusson tapestries we all, at the moment, imagine will be necessary for Lucy's trousseau.

Yesterday when I had dressed her after the shower she ex-amined herself intently in my mirror and asked for a French plait. I sat behind her at the dressing table blow-drying her black hair, brushing it and plaiting it. When Lucy was born, Um Sabir covered all the mirrors. His sister said, "They say if a baby looks in the mirror she will see her own grave." We laughed but did not remove the covers; they stayed in place till she was one.

I looked at Lucy's serious face in the mirror. I had seen my grave once, or thought I had. That was part of my Africa story. The plane out of Nigeria circled Cairo airport. Three times I heard the landing gear come down, and three times it was raised again. Sitting next to me were two Finnish businessmen. When the announcement came that we were rerouting to Luxor, they shook their heads and ordered another drink. At dawn, above Luxor airport, we were told there was trouble with the undercarriage and that the pilot was going to attempt a crash landing. I thought: so this is why they've sent us to Luxor, to burn up discreetly and not clog Cairo airport. We were asked to fasten our seat belts, take off our shoes and watches, put the cushions from the backs of our seats on our laps and bend double over them with our arms around our heads. I slung my handbag with my passport, tickets, and money around my neck and shoulder before I did these things. My Finnish neighbors formally shook each other's hands. On the plane there was perfect silence as we dropped out of the sky. And then a terrible, agonized, protracted screeching of machinery as we hit the tarmac. And in that moment, not only my head, but all of me, my whole being, seemed to tilt into a blank, an empty radiance, but lucid. Then three giant thoughts. One was of him—his name, over and over again. The other was of the children I would never have. The third was that the pattern was now complete: this is what my life amounted to.

When we did not die, that first thought—his name, his name, his name—became a talisman, for in extremity, hadn't all that was not him been wiped out of my life? My life, which once again stretched out before me, shimmering with possibilities, was meant to merge with his.

I finished the French plait and Lucy chose a blue clasp to secure its end. Before I let her run out, I smoothed some after-sun on her face. Her skin is nut-brown except just next to her ears, where it fades to a pale cream gleaming with golden down. I put my lips to her neck. "My Lucy, Lucia, *lambah,*" I murmured as I kissed her and let her go. My treasure, my trap.

Now when I walk to the sea, to the edge of this continent where I live, where I almost died, where I wait for my daughter to grow away from me, I see different things from those I saw that summer six years ago. The last of the foam is swallowed bubbling into the sand, to sink down and rejoin the sea at an invisible subterranean level. With each ebb of green water the sand loses part of itself to the sea; with each flow another part is flung back to be reclaimed once again by the beach. That narrow stretch of sand knows nothing in the world better than it does the white waves that whip it, caress it, collapse onto it, vanish into it. The white foam knows nothing better than those sands that wait for it, rise to it, and suck it in. But what do the waves know of the massed hot, still sands of the desert just twenty—no, ten feet beyond the scalloped edge? And what does the beach know of the depths, the cold, the currents just there, there—do you see it?—where the water turns a deeper blue.